PADDINGTON™
IN PERU

PADDINGTON™ IN PERU

THE STORY OF THE MOVIE

ANNA WILSON

HARPERCOLLINS
CHILDREN'S BOOKS

First published in the United Kingdom by
HarperCollins *Children's Books* in 2024
HarperCollins *Children's Books* is a division of HarperCollins*Publishers* Ltd
1 London Bridge Street
London SE1 9GF

www.harpercollins.co.uk

HarperCollins*Publishers*
Macken House, 39/40 Mayor Street Upper,
Dublin 1, D01 C9W8, Ireland

1

Written by Anna Wilson
Based on the story by Paul King, Mark Burton and Simon Farnaby
and the screenplay by Mark Burton, Jon Foster and James Lamont

Based on the Paddington novels written and created by Michael Bond

Copyright © P&Co. Ltd./SC 2024
Licensed on behalf of Studiocanal S.A.S. by Copyrights Group

ISBN 978-0-00-868180-7

Additional decorative icons used under licence from Shutterstock: Liena10
(guitar); imGhani (magnifying glass); Look_Studio (book); Swill Klitch (glasses);
Dasha Yahmina (ship's wheel); SofiaV (retro control buttons);
Studio_G (paintbrush and pot)

A CIP catalogue record for this title is available from the British Library.

Typeset in Stempel Garamond
by Palimpsest Book Production Ltd, Falkirk, Stirlingshire

Printed and bound in the UK using 100% renewable electricity
at CPI Group (UK) Ltd

This book contains FSC™ certified paper and other controlled
sources to ensure responsible forest management.

For more information visit: www.harpercollins.co.uk/green

CONTENTS

PROLOGUE

A few bear years ago, far away in Peru, *something* was rustling.

The "something" was hidden by tall plants in the lush cloud-forest undergrowth. Suddenly it stopped . . . and sniffed . . . and popped its head out of the greenery. It was . . . a little bear cub wearing a large red tropical flower as a hat! Right in front of the cub's nose hung a beautiful golden orange. The bear's eyes widened at the sight of the juicy fruit.

The orange was at the end of a long, thin branch. And it hung over a very steep slope!

Even so, the temptation to pick the fruit was just too much for the bear cub, so he started climbing towards it. He could almost reach it now. If he could just stretch a bit further . . .

CRACK!

The branch SNAPPED and . . .

"AAARGH!"

The cub tumbled down the steep slope.

"Oof! Yowch! Eeek!" cried the cub.

SPLOSH!

He landed in a mountain stream and was carried swiftly along by the current. He tried to grab at the grassy banks . . . but the water was flowing too fast.

Then suddenly . . .

WHOOMPF!

The little bear was plunged into darkness. He had entered a volcanic tunnel!

"ROOOOOAR!" The poor cub let out a feeble roar that echoed as he was propelled down twists and turns, towards a light that was getting bigger and bigger until . . .

WHOOSH!

He shot straight out of a hole in a cliffside

and landed in a much bigger river! He gasped
for air as the waters foamed around him, only
managing to keep afloat by desperately clinging
to a log.

The sun was setting now, and the river was
winding on through an impossibly steep-sided
canyon. The poor little cub clung to his log,
looking worriedly around him.

"Rooooooar . . .?" He shivered, realising how
tiny he was against the vast landscape.

Eventually he fell asleep on his log as the
mighty river carried him further and further
away from home.

Suddenly the waters became choppy again
and the bear cub was jolted awake by a
roaring sound, which was getting louder and
louder. The little cub's face filled with terror as
he realised it was the sound of a giant
waterfall to which he was drawing closer by
the second! A wave knocked him off his log.
He coughed and spluttered as he struggled to
keep afloat. He was sinking beneath the waves,
panicking, when . . .

"ROOOAR!" he cried as an adult bear reached out and grasped hold of his paw, pulling him up and out of the water.

The adult bear introduced herself as Aunt Lucy. She took the cub to her lovely rainforest treehouse and tucked him up cosily under a blanket. She gave him a marmalade sandwich, which he took gratefully as he was very hungry.

"Wherever did you come from?" Aunt Lucy asked.

The little cub said nothing, and just munched happily on the sandwich.

"Well, you are here now," said Aunt Lucy.

The cub swallowed and let out a very cute roar.

Aunt Lucy smiled. "That's it!" she said. "If you ever get lost again, just roar and I'll roar back. And I'll hear you . . . however far away you are . . ."

CHAPTER ONE

"SMILE, PLEASE!"

Some bear years later, that same little cub had grown up and was living in London with a family called the Browns . . .

Paddington Station was full of scurrying commuters. Everyone was much too busy to notice a strange squeaking noise coming from a photo booth. In any case, the photo booth seemed empty . . . until a bear's head came into view. It was Paddington! He was concentrating on raising the stool to the right height.

"A little too high . . ." He made some more adjustments. "A little lower . . . Ah! Perfect."

Paddington took a pound coin from his ear.
It had rather a lot of earwax on it, but he put
it into the machine anyway. Then – POP! –
the coin shot back out of the "reject" slot.
Paddington frowned and tried again. POP!
The same thing happened.

Oh dear. Paddington blew on the coin. *How
about I give it a "special rub" between my
paws?* he thought.

He put the coin in again and this time –
CLUNK – success! The machine hummed into
life and a pleasant recorded voice said, "Thank
you for using Photo-Me."

"Oh, not at all," said Paddington. "Thank
you for having me."

Paddington carefully adjusted his hat and
posed rather stiffly.

"Please note that headwear is not permitted,"
said the recorded voice.

"Isn't it?" Paddington quickly removed his
hat and posed again.

"Please note that headwear is not permitted,"
the recorded voice repeated.

"Oh?" Paddington was confused. He reached

up and realised that his emergency marmalade sandwich was still on his head, so he whipped it off and ate it.

The recorded voice spoke again. "Make sure your face is within the red circle."

Paddington frowned. "Pardon?"

"Commencing photos in 3 . . . 2 . . . 1 . . ."

Paddington hastily leaned forward and pressed his face right up against the red circle on the glass.

FLASH!

The camera had taken a photo of Paddington's face looking very squished! Paddington was so confused he fell back and spun round on the stool, making it rotate downwards so that he disappeared out of sight.

FLASH!

The camera had taken a photo of Paddington's bottom! He picked himself up, looking very messy.

"Wait!" he cried as he put the stool back up to the right height. But he spun the seat too quickly and the stool came free in his hand! *Oh no, now what?* he thought, just as the third flash blinded him.

He fell, his arm flailing in the air as he tried to pick up the stool, but it was stuck – the leg of the stool had jammed itself into the money slot.

FLASH!

The last photo was a blurred shot of the very top of Paddington's head. He wrenched the stool free, and the money-box cover came away with it! Coins cascaded all over the photo booth. Paddington was horrified. As he tried to feed the coins back into the slot, the recorded voice began speaking again.

"You have paid for twelve . . . twenty-six . . . forty-eight photos . . ."

The photo booth began rocking and flashing uncontrollably. Paddington whisked the curtain aside and stumbled out, totally blinded.

CRASH!

He immediately fell into a nearby newspaper kiosk and ended up on the floor in a heap of newspapers. But, surfacing from the pile, he was relieved to find a strip of passport photos in his paw – even if he did look a bit squashed in the photos.

CHAPTER TWO

LIFE WITH THE BROWNS

B ack in his attic room at 32 Windsor Gardens in London, Paddington was writing a letter.

Dear Aunt Lucy,

I am writing to you with some Very Important News! This morning, Joe the postman delivered a very exciting envelope. Mr and Mrs Brown and all our neighbours were there to see me open it.

You'll never guess what it was . . . My very own British passport! Everyone gave me a round of applause. Mr Brown said, "Now you can 'Pass Freely Without Let or Hindrance'." So, Aunt Lucy, this means that I am now "Officially British"! Like crumpets – or queuing – or saying "Crikey!".

All my friends had kindly chipped in to buy me a gift. It was a very smart black umbrella, tied up with a bow. Dr Jafri said, "No British gentleman should be without an umbrella." And Colonel Lancaster told me that it was, "Not just any brolly – it's the 'Windsorman Deluxe', London's finest." I thanked them all very much. When I clicked a button on the handle, it made an impressive sound and sprang open! Everyone gasped!

I cannot tell you how proud I am to be Officially British . . .

There have been a few other changes at Windsor Gardens since you were last here . . . Judy is applying to university, a process which is known as "flying the nest". This involves visiting a place called a "campus".

Apparently, you have to take a parent with you, so there's someone to cry at the thought of you leaving home. However, it seems that Mrs Brown cried a little too much, so Judy asked if she could bring Mr Brown next time. The trouble is he ended up crying as well. But it didn't matter too much as, according to Judy, all the visiting parents were sobbing.

Jonathan, on the other hand, rarely leaves his room. He spends most of his time "chillin'" (the "g" is silent). He has put a lot of effort into doing as little as possible, which is why he's invented "The Bicy-chill", a cross between a bicycle and an armchair. He's also invented something called "The Gobsleigh", which is a very clever invention that delivers snacks from the fridge via a little ski-jump, right into Jonathan's mouth (or "gob", as he calls it). Then there is his most prized creation, the "Snack Hack", which involves a robotic arm coming out of his wardrobe to drop yet another snack into his lap. It also sprays him with deodorant. That invention is still "patent pending". Mr Brown thinks that maybe it's time to take "these ingenious gizmos" out of Jonathan's bedroom and into the real world.

Mrs Brown says it's brilliant that the kids have grown up because now she's got lots of time for her new art project. It is a collage of Jonathan and Judy as little children playing on the sofa. It's called "The Sofa Years" because of the time when the whole family could all fit on one sofa.

Mr Brown remembers that during those years he didn't ever finish a single crossword, but now he finishes them all the time. Mind you, he has to spend a lot of time at work at the moment because he's got a new boss – an American called Madison. He has to have breakfast meetings before work where he "connects" with Madison. She thinks the company needs something called a "shake-up". She says that Mr Brown needs to "embrace the risk!" like her assistant Zayden, who paraglides into the office with her coffee in the morning. Mr Brown is not sure that he can do this.

Meanwhile, Mrs Bird has finally found some time to tick things off her "to-do" list. She has got rid of the wasp nest that was in the house and has fixed the ancient fuse box without too many explosions . . .

However, the biggest change at Windsor Gardens is that, despite the Browns living in the same house, they don't actually seem to spend much time together any more. But life in London is still quite wonderful and I feel very much at home.

Lots of love,
Paddington

Suddenly Mrs Brown appeared at the foot of the attic stairs, holding a letter.

"Paddington! There's another letter for you!" she said. "I think it's from Aunt Lucy."

Paddington took the letter and opened it, feeling puzzled. "But . . . this isn't Aunt Lucy's handwriting . . ." He started reading aloud:

"*Dear Paddington, please forgive my contacting you. We haven't met, but I'm the Reverend Mother at the Home for Retired Bears in Peru. I'm afraid I have some rather worrying news about your Aunt Lucy . . .*"

Paddington looked up, his face creased with concern. "Oh . . ." he said.

Mrs Brown encouraged him to keep reading.

Paddington continued. "*She's always been such a happy member of our community. So bright and full of life! She has sung with the nuns' choir, for example. But now there's been the most pronounced change. She spends hours alone in her room. She seems to be missing you desperately! Please don't mention I wrote. She wouldn't want you bothered by such things. But, as the Lord tells us, 'The do-er who acts will be blessed in the doing.' So I felt I must tell you – something is not right with Aunt Lucy. Yours sincerely, Reverend Mother.*"

Later that day, Paddington read the letter out again to the whole family. "Something's not right with Aunt Lucy," he said. "I had no idea!"

The Browns reacted with sympathy and concern.

"Oh, Paddington." Mrs Brown sighed. "She must really be missing you."

"I can't bear to think of her feeling lonely," said Paddington anxiously. "After all she's done for me . . . What can we do?"

"Well, I'm not sure there's much we *can* do. It's not like we can drop everything and fly to Peru!" said Mr Brown, laughing at the thought.

Mrs Brown's eyes lit up with excitement.

Mr Brown became worried. "Mary . . . I know that look!"

"It's the perfect idea!" Mrs Brown interrupted. "Aunt Lucy's missing Paddington, he's just got his passport, this family *needs* to spend more time together . . ."

"Does it?" asked Jonathan.

"Let's do it!" cried Mrs Brown.

"A trip to Peru!" Judy exclaimed.

"A *family* holiday to Peru," said Mrs Brown firmly.

"Peru?" said Mr Brown, looking shocked.

"Just like that? Land of altitude sickness, uncharted jungles . . .'

Mrs Bird raised her eyebrows. "And three of the world's most dangerous roads, at least on a Harley . . ."

"Precisely!" said Mr Brown. "From a risk-assessment point of view Peru is . . ." He tailed off as something dawned on him. He thought of his new boss, Madison, and her cool assistant, Zayden. What was it Madison had said? *Embrace the risk, Henry . . .* ". . . Peru is *exactly* where we should be going," he finished.

The whole family looked at him in astonishment, and Paddington beamed as he realised what this meant. He rushed back to add a P.S. to his letter to Aunt Lucy:

P.S. There is actually some more very important news! <u>WE'RE COMING TO VISIT YOU. THE BROWNS ARE COMING TO PERU!!!!</u>

CHAPTER THREE

PREPARING FOR PADDINGTON!

A few bear days later, in the Home for Retired Bears in Peru, the Reverend Mother was strumming the tune to *"Kumbaya"* on her Spanish guitar when Aunt Lucy burst in excitedly, clutching her letter from Paddington.

"My nephew, Paddington – he's coming to visit! He's coming here to the Home for Retired Bears, completely out of the blue!"

The Reverend Mother gave a gasp. "Hallelujah!" she cried and strummed another chord on her guitar.

Taking the instrument with her, she strode out of her office and into the cloisters.

"Get ready, everyone!" she called out. "He's coming!" The nuns looked up from their chores as the Reverend Mother sang out, *"Let's prepare for Paddington – Paddington in Peru!"*

A number of nuns followed her along the cloisters and joined in her singing. Aunt Lucy came up behind them, feeling slightly bewildered.

"He's coming to stay from far away . . ." sang the Reverend Mother.

"And there's so much to do!" sang the nuns.

"There's prepping and there's packing," the Reverend Mother continued.

"No plan must be lacking," the nuns sang.

"There's no time for slacking. We'd better get cracking . . ." the Reverend Mother went on as a larger group of nuns appeared. They reached the end of the cloisters, just as the nuns chorused, *". . . and bring your nephew to you!"*

BONG!

A nun rang the chapel bell as the procession entered the large common room where retired bears sat about relaxing, playing dominoes, reading the paper or knitting. They looked up, a little confused by all the sudden jollity.

"*Let's prepare for Paddington, Paddington in Peru!*" sang the nuns.

More nuns joined in with harmonies and tambourines, while others began to dust, polish and vacuum in time to the music.

An old bear reading the paper asked, "Can he get me some duty free?"

Nuns appeared on roller-skates, singing while they glided around the common room, while others performed a tap dance. Some were juggling badminton rackets and oranges! One of the bears clicked her knitting needles rhythmically in time to the music as she held up a square of knitting that showed a picture of Paddington's face. A nun beat out a rhythm on a dusty rug using a rug-beater, while yet another ran up a wall and performed a somersault! Then a nun playing the organ changed suddenly from traditional hymns to an impressive heavy rock solo!

The nuns were building to the grand finale of their song now: "*Everything must go with* a swing," they chorused, *"for Paddington in Peru! Let's prepare for Paddington, Paddington in Peru . . ."*

They danced down some steps and out of the front entrance of the Home for Retired Bears, then on to the front lawn, still singing: *"Paddington . . ."*

Then the Reverend Mother ran out and threw her guitar high into the air. Still singing, she pirouetted again and again, the beautiful mountains all around her, a huge smile on her face. Then she flung her arms wide, and her guitar dropped from the heavens into her hands.

"Paddington in Peruuuuuu . . ." She took a huge breath for the last line: *"Paddington in Peru!"*

The song ended triumphantly, just as there was a warning rumble of thunder in the distance . . .

Meanwhile, back in London, everyone was busy getting ready for the trip.

Mrs Brown was packing her art materials. She found an old game of Travel Scrabble. *That might come in useful*, she thought. Smiling, she added it to the contents of her suitcase.

Mr Brown was hurrying along the aisles of his local pharmacy, sweeping giant cans of anti-bug spray, medicines and sunscreen into his basket. He suddenly noticed a pair of cool sunglasses . . . They were a bit like the ones Zayden wore . . .

Maybe they will suit the new adventurous me, Mr Brown thought. He abandoned his basketful of sensible shopping and just bought the sunglasses instead.

Paddington was in the attic doing his own spot of packing. He unfolded two travel toothbrushes and inspected them curiously. Then he tested them both in his ears. *Perfect!* he thought as he folded them back up and put them in his suitcase.

Judy was throwing some new notebooks and a camera into her bag. She found her old Dictaphone as well and pressed a button to see if it still worked. "Nice buns!" said a familiar voice.

"Yup, still working." Judy nodded approvingly.

Jonathan was playing video games while his "Snack Hack" packed his bag for him. It picked up some boxer shorts and automatically sprayed them with "Teenage Boy" deodorant. Then it packed the deodorant too!

Mrs Bird opened her suitcase, put a toolbox inside and then shut it. She didn't seem to think she would need anything else!

The Browns and Mrs Bird all shut their suitcases one after the other.

CLICK!

CLICK!

CLICK!

CLICK!

CLICK!

Paddington's suitcase was filled to the brim with jars of marmalade. He forced the lid shut by sitting on it . . . and then bumped down the stairs, riding on his suitcase.

They were ready to go to Peru!

CHAPTER FOUR

A STRANGE STATUE

A short while later . . .

Mr Gruber and Paddington were sitting inside Gruber's Antiques on the Portobello Road, enjoying a pot of tea together while the rain pelted against the windows. A storm was blowing outside, but inside the shop it was cosy and warm.

"Paddington in Peru, eh?" said Mr Gruber. "That sounds splendid. When are you off?"

"First thing tomorrow!" Paddington replied. "Did you know there was such a thing as 'six o'clock in the morning', Mr Gruber?" He was

rather overexcited. "I can't wait to see Aunt Lucy – and try *this* out, of course."
Paddington pushed his shiny new passport over to Mr Gruber.

Mr Gruber opened it. He looked rather surprised when he saw the photo of Paddington's squished face and his funny expression.

"I'm Officially British now, you know!" Paddington was saying. He held his teacup delicately, his little furry finger pointing out in an unusually refined manner. Then he promptly gulped the tea down, poured the milk into his mouth straight from the jug and tossed in some sugar cubes!

"And not before time," said Mr Gruber approvingly. "We are very lucky to have you, Mr Brown!" He had a sudden thought. "Oh! I have something for Judy . . . for your trip." Mr Gruber disappeared into the back of his shop and called out over his shoulder, "Help yourself to a bun."

As Paddington ate his bun, he found himself drawn to a small wooden bear statue in the middle of a bookshelf. He approached the statue, staring at it, and the statue peered back at him. Paddington looked even more closely. Then, suddenly . . .

KA-BOOM!

A flash of lightning from the storm outside lit up the shop, and . . . the statue seemed to come alive for a moment and roared!

"RORRRAGH!"

Paddington gasped. He saw a flash of golden light, a splash of water, and for a split second he wasn't in Mr Gruber's shop any more. Instead, he was back in the deep, dense rainforest of his homeland.

Mr Gruber returned from his storeroom holding a vintage book. "A guidebook to Peru for Judy!" he said. His voice snapped Paddington out of his strange trance. "It is somewhat old, perhaps," Mr Gruber went on. "Ignore the chapter on 'Zeppelin Travel' . . ."

Mr Gruber looked up to see Paddington frozen in shock. "Mr Brown?" Mr Gruber asked. "Have you been seeing a ghost?"

"Mr Gruber . . . that statue . . ." Paddington stammered. "What is it?"

"It is one of my South American bob-a-ma-
things," said Mr Gruber, examining it. "Oh, it
is coming from Peru, like you."

Paddington said, "It just . . . ROARED!
Like it was . . . speaking to me?"

Mr Gruber regarded the statue – it clearly was
only a statue and could not have spoken. But he
smiled at Paddington and said, "I understand,
Mr Brown. Things from my homeland speak to
me all the time."

Paddington frowned. "It was very strange,
Mr Gruber . . ."

Mr Gruber looked thoughtful for a moment,
then he glanced again at Paddington's passport.
"Mr Brown . . . you know, becoming a citizen
of a new country, while a wonderful thing, can
lead to . . . well, mixed feelings."

Paddington picked up his passport. He
looked unsure. "Oh, not me, Mr Gruber . . .
my feelings are very much unmixed."

Mr Gruber did not seem convinced.

Paddington looked at the statue again. "You
said it was from Peru. I think I'll speak to Aunt
Lucy about it – she'll know what it means."

He turned to leave – but Mr Gruber stopped him. "Paddington! Your umbrella!"

"Oh, yes!" said Paddington. "Mustn't leave my Windsorman Deluxe. After all, I *am* going to a rainforest . . ."

CHAPTER FIVE

TIME FOR TAKE-OFF!

The Browns and Paddington were off to Peru!

On the plane, Barry the air steward was leading them in the safety demonstration. "Make sure your tray table is securely stowed . . ." he was saying.

Paddington obediently put up his table.

"And your seatbelt securely fastened . . ." Barry continued.

Paddington clipped his belt.

Barry went on to demonstrate how the life jacket worked: ". . . pull the red cord to inflate your life jacket . . ."

28

Paddington had somehow managed to put on his life jacket, even though he was still sitting in his seat. He thought he should obey Barry's instruction, so he pulled the red cord and . . .WHOOMPH! The lifejacket instantly inflated.

Barry looked shocked.

"They didn't mean *now*, Paddington!" said Mr Brown.

A few hours later, the plane landed in Lima. When Paddington showed his passport, the officer behind the glass partition frowned at the squished face in the photo, just as Mr Gruber had done. Then he looked back at Paddington, confused. Paddington quickly pulled a silly face and squished his face up against the glass so that it matched his face in the photo. The officer nodded and seemed satisfied that it was indeed Paddington's passport. He stamped it then waved him through.

The Brown family took a little yellow and white taxi-bus from Lima airport and went through the main square of the city, which was bustling with activity. People in colourful clothing were selling rainbow-striped fabrics, hats, bags and musical instruments. There were mountainous piles of all kinds of fruit and vegetables and there was a lot of joyful shouting as the stallholders called out to passers-by to tempt them to buy their wares. The Browns passed a band of musicians dressed in beautiful red jackets and little black hats. They were playing wonderful lively music.

The Browns soon left the town and continued their journey along a desert road. Paddington opened the window to take in the sights. The breathtaking green Andes mountains rose up into a clear blue sky, their tops dusted with snow. The road wound alongside a crystal-blue river and lush green fields in which flocks of llamas were grazing. The road went up and up into the mountains, taking the taxi along a very narrow road on a cliff-edge above an incredibly steep, rather scary drop.

"Nice view, huh?" asked the taxi driver.

Mr Brown peered out of the window in

terror and whispered to himself, "Embrace the risk . . . embrace the risk . . ." He flipped down his "cool" sunglasses and tried to remain calm, but he was terrified by how high they were going.

Meanwhile Judy was talking into her Dictaphone, flicking through her vintage guidebook. "Peru Travelogue, day one," she said. "To understand Peru, you must know its history . . . First came the Incas, who built Machu Picchu and other great cities in the jungle . . . Then came the Spanish Conquest, in which tall ships crossed the ocean with men seeking gold. The greediest of all of these was a man called Gonzalo Caboto, who was desperate to find a legendary place called El Dorado . . ."

Jonathan leaned in and interrupted. "You mean that piri-piri chicken shop on Edgware Road?" he asked.

Judy snapped off the Dictaphone impatiently. "This is for my uni application! It's really competitive!"

Jonathan rolled his eyes. "Sounds like effort."

*　*　*

They stopped for a break and Paddington posed while Judy took a photo of him with a small crowd of smiling Peruvian village children. Paddington politely raised his hat to a passing llama – and it promptly ate his marmalade sandwich! Then he and the Browns got back into the taxi-bus, and it took them down out of the mountains. The road was long and winding, and Paddington was soon fast asleep.

He was stirred from his slumber sometime later by a familiar scent. He pushed his snout through the open window to take a bigger sniff and let out a low contented growl. He recognised the smell: it was the Amazon rainforest, which stretched endlessly into the distance.

Mr Brown was not looking out of the window. Instead, he was nose-deep in a *Risk Manual of Peru*.

"Why have you brought that?" Mrs Brown asked. "I thought you were supposed to be 'embracing risk'?"

Mr Brown looked embarrassed. "I am! I'm

just . . . researching which risk to embrace first." He went back to his book, which showed a huge spider called a "purple-kneed tarantula". "Actual size," he muttered to himself in horror.

"I think we're here!" Mrs Brown cried as the taxi-bus slowed to a stop.

Paddington pressed his face and paws against the window in excitement. He stared out at a low, cosy-looking building, peacefully nestled in the trees. It had a neat, thatched roof and steps leading up to a cool, shaded entrance where two nuns were standing smiling. They were dressed in long, dark-blue habits and white headdresses. Next to this house was a simple white church with a bell tower and a red-tiled roof. Nuns came and went from the church along a dusty path, smiling and chatting, and old bears rested on sun loungers under colourful parasols. There was a welcoming sign that read: "Home for Retired Bears".

The door practically fell off its hinges as Paddington leaped out of the taxi-bus and ran up the steps.

"Aunt Lucy, we're here!" he cried.

Mr and Mrs Brown stumbled out behind Paddington, rubbing their sore backs, with Judy, Jonathan and Mrs Bird following. The Reverend Mother approached them with a serious look on her face. But Paddington hurried past her towards the cabins, clutching his hat and calling out, "Aunt Lucy!" He rushed on past two nuns, raising his hat politely. "Hello, good afternoon!" he said. He didn't notice them exchange a look of concern. Eventually Paddington found a cabin with Aunt Lucy's name on it and ran up to the door, crying, "Aunt Lucy, it's me!" as he burst inside.

But . . . it was empty.

Paddington was puzzled. "Aunt Lucy?" he said as he looked around her neat and tidy room. He quickly checked the wardrobe. He even checked under the bed. There was no sign of her.

When he got back to his feet, he saw that the Browns had appeared at the door, accompanied by the Reverend Mother.

"I . . . I'm afraid there's some bad news," she said, looking grave.

Paddington glanced at Mrs Brown, who looked worried. Then he saw that all the Browns had the same expression, and he began to feel more and more anxious by the minute.

CHAPTER SIX

A WORRYING TURN OF EVENTS

Paddington and the Browns followed the Reverend Mother into her office. They sat down opposite her and her silent assistant, Rosita.

"Missing?" Paddington repeated. "Whatever do you mean?"

The Reverend Mother looked at Paddington, her hands clasped. "Just that," she said. "She's gone. And we have no idea where she is."

The Browns looked at one another, confused.

"What do you mean 'gone'?" asked Mr Brown.

"She seems to have set off on some kind of quest into the jungle," explained the Reverend Mother.

"Now?" said Paddington. "But she knew we were coming!"

The Reverend Mother nodded. "That's what's so mysterious. She was very excited about seeing you and she was counting the days to your arrival." She sighed thoughtfully, then went on. "But I'm afraid to say that, since I wrote to you, your aunt's behaviour has become even more worrying. She seemed to be researching something. Whatever it was, she was obsessed with it . . . She wouldn't let me see what it was she was working on. She was very secretive about the whole thing. Then last night Rosita and I went to check on her – and she wasn't there."

Paddington paced anxiously. "This isn't like Aunt Lucy. Something's wrong. We need to send out a search party!"

The Reverend Mother produced a small cardboard box. "We already did, my dear," she said sadly. "All they found were these, washed down the river."

Paddington was filled with dread as he pulled out Aunt Lucy's bracelet – it was made of strands of coloured string knotted together and had a talisman of a bear threaded on to it. The bracelet was covered in mud.

"Aunt Lucy's bracelet!" said Paddington. "She'd never take this off, unless—" He stopped himself. Then he noticed something else in the box. He fished out Aunt Lucy's broken glasses. The others gasped.

"Oh dear," said Mr Brown.

The Browns exchanged a hurried glance. Things did not look good.

"Oh no, Paddington!" said Mrs Brown.

"I don't know what's happened to her, Mrs Brown," said Paddington, "but she's out there. She may be hurt, or in trouble. She can't see without her glasses and I . . . I have to find her." He sounded so worried.

Mr Brown glanced over at a large wall map of the Amazon. He put a comforting hand on Paddington's shoulder. "Look, Paddington," he said, "I hate to say this, but the Amazon is quite . . ."

Rosita interrupted him by turning a little handle next to the map. A pair of wooden panels slowly slid apart, revealing even more of the map.

Paddington looked at it in awe.

". . . large," finished Mr Brown, hopelessly.

Rosita started turning the handle again and the panels pulled back further to reveal even more of the map. The Reverend Mother gave a discreet shake of her head to make it clear to Rosita that she was not helping. Seeing how big the Amazon really was made Paddington even more anxious.

He turned to face the others, his big brown eyes wet with tears. "We have to try," he insisted. "She would never give up on me."

"Paddington," Mrs Brown said gently, "the answer to *one* bear getting lost is not *another* bear getting even more lost."

The Reverend Mother agreed. "Alas, there's nothing any of us can do tonight. And you must be tired after your journey. Our path will be clearer in the morning. The nuns will show you to your rooms."

Paddington nodded miserably.

The Browns shuffled out, with Paddington behind them. The Reverend Mother put her hand on his arm.

"All it takes to light the darkness is one candle of faith," she said. "Something will turn up."

Paddington smiled weakly. "Thank you, Reverend Mother," he said. Then he left, gently closing the door behind him.

"So sad," said the Reverend Mother, picking up her guitar and strumming a mournful chord.

Back in Aunt Lucy's cabin, Paddington struck a match in the darkness. It lit up his worried expression.

"Where are you, Aunt Lucy?" he asked. He looked at Aunt Lucy's bracelet, which he was now wearing himself. Then he went to light a candle on Aunt Lucy's desk. "What were you looking for?" he continued. "If only you had left me some sort of clue . . ."

The candle cast a shaft of light across the room, which landed directly on a framed picture on the wall of Aunt Lucy with a younger Paddington. There was a document tucked in behind the picture!

"Oh, my goodness!" he cried. "This must be it!" But Paddington had not seen the document. Instead he was fiddling with a floorboard. "This floorboard's loose!" he said. "Perhaps there's a secret compartment or . . ." He stamped on the floorboard to loosen it, but it catapulted up and hit him straight in the face!

He tumbled across the room, banging into the wall. This caused the document to come free from behind the picture and it landed in his lap. He unfolded it carefully, his eyes widening . . .

CHAPTER SEVEN

THE HUNT BEGINS

The next morning, Mr Brown went to the reception of the Home for Retired Bears to make a phone call.

"I'd like to report a missing bear, please . . . Umm, about five foot two, brown eyes, brown fur . . . in fact, just brown . . . in the jungle . . . Yes, we've lost a jungle bear in the jungle." He frowned. "I'm not sure I like your tone!" he added.

The rest of the Brown family were glumly picking at their breakfast as Mr Brown came back into the room.

"Any luck with the police?" Mrs Brown asked.

Mr Brown looked fed up. "Apparently, they are 'too busy looking for lost fish in the river'," he said with heavy sarcasm.

Mrs Bird was by the breakfast bar. She started bobbing up and down, bending her knees.

"Everything all right, Mrs Bird?" asked Judy.

"I've got that twinge in my knees," Mrs Bird explained. "There's something odd about Aunt Lucy leaving like that with no explanation." She looked uncertainly at Rosita and the other nuns at the breakfast bar.

Paddington suddenly appeared, full of energy. "Morning, everyone. I know where Aunt Lucy's gone!" He slammed down an ancient-looking chart. It was a hand-drawn map of the Amazon. He tapped it with authority and said, "It's a place called Rumi Rock, and it's only a few days upriver."

The Browns were stunned into silence. Paddington slapped some marmalade on a sandwich and popped it under his hat. "We can take breakfast with us," he said.

"Wait, wait! Paddington, what's going on?

Where did you get this old map?" asked Mrs Brown.

"I found it in Aunt Lucy's room," said Paddington. "In fact, I rather think she *wanted* me to find it."

"Rumi Rock? What makes you think we should start the search there?" asked Mr Brown.

Judy was studying the map. "Well, Aunt Lucy has made a note," she said, pointing. "'Start search here,' it says." The words were scribbled in Aunt Lucy's handwriting, right next to a spot in the jungle labelled "Rumi Rock" which she seemed to have circled.

The Browns exchanged an intrigued glance.

They took the chart straight to the Reverend Mother. She picked up a magnifying glass and studied the map carefully. "The Lord be praised!" she cried. "I knew something would turn up."

"What is this 'Rumi Rock'?" asked Mr Brown.

"It's a sacred Inca stone circle deep in the jungle," the Reverend Mother explained.

"What's so special about it?" asked Mrs Brown.

The Reverend Mother shrugged. "No idea. Sacred Inca monuments are not really a nun thing." She put her hand on Paddington's paw. "But," she continued, sounding excited, "it's a clue to finding Aunt Lucy. Seek out what she was looking for and it may lead you to her. If anyone can do it, it's you, young bear."

Paddington was looking thoughtful. "Aunt Lucy always says, 'When skies are grey, hope is the way.' A long time ago, she found me. Now it's my turn to find her."

Mr Brown butted in. "Now hang on a minute – surely someone *here* –" he looked pointedly at the Reverend Mother – "would be in a better position to . . ."

The Reverend Mother shook her head sadly. "I no longer permit myself or my nuns to enter the jungle," she said, "because I find it somewhat . . ." She broke off and glanced anxiously at a painting high up on her office wall. She hesitated, her eyes roaming over the image of mysterious creatures made of leaves. "It's best I stay here and tend my flock," she said eventually. "But I commend your bravery and have faith you will survive!"

Mrs Bird shot a doubtful glance sideways at Mrs Brown.

"Well, that's reassuring," said Mr Brown.

"Mr Brown," said Paddington, making himself brave, "if you feel you can't come, I shall go on my own."

Mrs Brown looked pointedly at her husband.

"Right," said Mr Brown, giving in. It was clear the decision had been made for him. "Obviously the Brown family are exactly the right people – with *all* the requisite skills – to go and find a lost bear in the jungle."

"Thank you, Mr Brown," said Paddington.

The Reverend Mother produced her guitar and strummed a chord. "Hallelujah! And don't forget these . . ." She handed Paddington Aunt Lucy's glasses. "You can give them to your aunt when you find her," she said.

"Thank you very much," said Paddington.

"Maybe someone should, like, chill here," suggested Jonathan, "in case Aunt Lucy comes back?"

"Aye," said Mrs Bird. "I'll man base camp and make sure everything's shipshape for when she returns." She turned to the Reverend Mother. "I had a peek at your fuse board. Rustier than my grandmother's bedpan."

The Reverend Mother looked shocked and said, "No need for that, Mrs Bird. Better for you to relax."

The Browns were about to leave when the Reverend Mother took Mrs Brown aside. "Oh, Mary – just one thing . . ."

Mrs Brown paused, and turned round to see the Reverend Mother was holding out a silver St Christopher medallion on a chain.

"Forgive an old nun her comforts . . ." The Reverend Mother slipped the chain over Mrs Brown's head. "St Christopher, the patron saint of travel. I truly believe he will keep your family safe. Keep him close?"

Mrs Brown looked at the medallion round her neck. "Of course, Reverend Mother. Thank you. We need all the help we can get."

The Reverend Mother touched Mrs Brown's cheek and nodded gratefully.

CHAPTER EIGHT

THE BEST BOAT ON THE RIVER

Later that day, Paddington and the Browns were making their way through a bustling marketplace at the docks. It was full of stalls selling all sorts of things from boat equipment to clothes to food. There were piles and piles of all kinds of fruit and vegetables and freshly caught fish. There were tables covered in bolts of multicoloured fabrics, neatly folded ponchos, wide-brimmed Peruvian hats, beautiful bags made from woven material and rows and rows of brightly painted pottery.

Everything was very tempting, but today was not the day to go shopping.

"We just need to find a boat that will take us upriver," said Paddington.

As he was speaking, he saw someone walking towards him carrying a wooden canoe. The person turned sharply, and Paddington had to dive underneath the canoe before it hit him.

The Browns didn't notice. Mrs Brown was fussing over Judy and Jonathan, trying to smear their faces with sun cream. They were protesting loudly!

"I can do my own sun cream!" Judy cried.

". . . behind your ears!" Mrs Brown added, much to the children's annoyance.

Mr Brown puffed out his chest and strutted around, trying to sound tough. "Everyone, listen up! We are on the threshold of the actual Amazon – a place full of risk. So we're going to have to embrace that."

"Mr Brown, why are you walking like that?" asked Paddington.

Mrs Brown tried to bite back a smile. "It's his 'hard walk'," she explained.

Mr Brown looked offended. "It's a perfectly normal walk," he said.

Judy sniggered. "He does it when the plumber comes around."

"I do not!" said Mr Brown. He turned to address the family, the docks behind him. "Whatever boat we find, it's not exactly going to be the pride of the regatta, okay?"

At that moment, a beautiful vintage sailing boat cruised into view. Mr Brown had his back to it, so he didn't see it.

"Er, Mr Brown?" Paddington tried to get his attention, but Mr Brown wasn't listening.

"All I'm saying is: be prepared to row," Mr Brown went on.

Paddington pointed at the beautiful boat. "Mr Brown – look!"

Mr Brown turned round to see the boat, and his eyes widened. The boat was incredible! And on deck there was an elegant gentleman in a cream linen suit who seemed as if he might be the perfect captain.

"Ooh, what a handsome . . ." Mrs Brown

caught Mr Brown's eye and added quickly,
". . . boat."

"Ahoy there!" called the captain.

"Excuse me, sir?" said Paddington. "Is this
boat for hire?"

"For hire?" the man said, looking
surprised. "Señor Bear, it is your lucky day!"
He glided effortlessly across the deck. He
hopped nimbly forward on to the jetty, tied
up the boat with a flourish and came to shake
Paddington by the paw.

"This is the best boat on the river!" The
captain patted the boat, and a porthole
window swung awkwardly from its hinge.
He cleared his throat and quickly shut the
porthole.

Mr Brown raised an eyebrow at his wife, but
she had not noticed the broken porthole.

"Part of the charm," said the captain hastily.
He looked wistfully at his boat and ran his
hand along it. "Strong, smooth, not so bad on
the eyes. And that's just the boat!" He laughed
at his own joke, then said, "Captain Hunter

Cabot at your service." With that, he thumped the hull of the ship and shouted, "GINA!"

A young woman popped up from the engine room, holding a wrench. Her dungarees were covered in oil.

"My daughter, Gina," the captain explained. "Gina, these people are here for a tour!"

"TOUR? *¡Hola! ¡Buenos dias!*" she cried. "We have many tours available. We could see the pink dolphins?"

"Take in some Inca ruins?" Hunter chimed in.

"Feed the piranhas . . ." added Gina.

Then together they chorused: "Although it may cost you an arm and a leg!"

They both paused for a laugh that didn't come.

Paddington pulled out the map. "We need to go to somewhere called Rumi Rock."

The atmosphere darkened and Hunter and Gina's smiles faded.

". . . Rumi Rock?" Hunter repeated.

"We don't go to Rumi Rock," said Gina firmly.

Hunter said in an aside to Gina, "Gina, we could do with a tour . . ."

"We don't need this one," Gina replied.

Hunter sighed and turned to Paddington. "I'm sorry, little bear, but you'll have to take your sightseeing somewhere else."

Paddington was insistent. "No, we're not sightseers. It's an emergency. My Aunt Lucy has gone missing. Now she's out there somewhere, all alone."

"We don't go to Rumi Rock," said Gina even more firmly than before.

But Paddington was not giving up. "I'm her only family, and I've lost her. Please can you make an exception, just this once?"

Hunter looked at Gina and Gina looked at Paddington, his big brown eyes pleading.

A short time later, Gina was manoeuvring the boat into the river, while talking into the loudspeaker. "Welcome aboard for your once-in-a-lifetime, never-to-be-repeated trip to Rumi Rock."

As she said this, Hunter was fiddling with a gold signet ring on his finger, which had his family's crest engraved on it. He seemed distracted as the boat set sail upriver through the brightly coloured rainforest.

Judy began recording her travelogue again, speaking into her Dictaphone. "Day two. We head off the tourist trail and into the jungle – our fate in the hands of the charming Captain Cabot, who seems oddly familiar . . ."

Mr Brown was at the prow of the boat, staring out at the majestic Amazon River and the rich greens and blues of the rainforest and the sky. "Hey, Judy," he said, turning back to his daughter. He spread his arms, gesturing to the breathtaking view. "Take a photo with all this, for the dudes back at the office."

"Dudes?" Judy repeated, pulling a face.

"Just take the photo," said Mr Brown. He slipped on his new sunglasses, ready to pose for the picture.

Standing by the rail, Paddington was breathing in the jungle, full of wonder.

"Good to be back?" Mrs Brown asked him.

"It will be," said Paddington. "When we find Aunt Lucy." He looked out into the dense jungle on the nearby riverbank.

"What was it?" said Mrs Brown. "'When skies are . . .'?"

"'When skies are grey, hope is the way,'" said Paddington, desperately wishing it to be true.

CHAPTER NINE

MR BROWN TRIES TO BE BRAVE

"Your cabins are ready now!" Hunter said, appearing on deck. "Step where I step – to the inexperienced, a boat can pose many hazards –"

Gina suddenly shouted out, "BOOM!"

Hunter immediately ducked as a large boom pole swung across the deck. He stood up again. "Thanks, Gina!" he called back. Then, shaking his head, he said, "She has to warn me. Every time!" He swooped below deck, sliding down the ladder rungs smoothly and shouted, "Come below deck to your quarters!"

The Browns and Paddington followed Hunter down the ladder into the saloon. They admired the beautiful room. There was even a ship's piano in the corner! Hunter tinkled a quick tune for them. He was surprisingly good at it! Then he cheekily raised his hands to show that the instrument was in fact a "player-piano" – it could play tunes on its own without a pianist to play the keys!

Hunter stopped next to a large antique globe and gave it a spin. "En route to your destination," he said, "other stops can include . . ." The globe popped open to reveal a drinks cabinet inside. He held up a bottle of whisky, then rum. "Scotland . . . or even Jamaica!"

"Who are these people?" Judy asked.

There was a series of old framed photos and portraits on the wall featuring historical figures grouped around a coat of arms. All the people in the pictures looked very much like Hunter.

"Ah, those are my ancestors," Hunter said. "The Cabotos – they like to keep an eye on me," he added. He made his voice light and jokey and went on, "To make sure I bring glory to the family!"

Mrs Brown nodded to the coat of arms.
"That's like your tattoo," she said.

"Good spot, Mary," said Hunter.

Mr Brown eyed his wife. "What tattoo?"

"The fist of gold – the Cabot family crest,"
said Hunter, rolling up his sleeve to reveal it.

"Very observant," said Mr Brown. "Drunken
night in Cusco, was it?"

Hunter was suddenly serious. He gave the
piano a kick, so that it stopped playing. "No,"
he growled. "It is a badge of pride. ALL
Cabots have this tattoo."

Mr Brown looked embarrassed.

Hunter pulled up his shirt, cheerfully. "THIS
was a drunken night in Cusco," he said. Then
he opened the door to a spacious room. "And
finally – the Darwin Suite," he announced.

Mr and Mrs Brown peered inside. The walls
were decorated with stuffed animals in glass
cases and some framed drawings of plants. There
was a hat on a stand that looked like the type an
explorer would wear. Mr Brown stepped into the
room and looked around admiringly.

"Oh yes, this is quite— Whoa!" He had

come face to face with a stuffed purple-kneed tarantula in a glass case on the wall opposite the bed. "The old purple-kneed tarantula," he said, trying to sound as if he wasn't bothered by it.

Mrs Brown said, "My husband's got a bit of a thing about spiders. And bugs. In fact, he's got a whole folder—"

Mr Brown interrupted hastily. "DON'T bother the captain with all that, darling!" He was trying to act casual, but was clearly feeling very uncomfortable.

"Maybe I should . . . remove it?" Hunter suggested.

Mr Brown tried to cover up his nerves and sound brave. "No, no! Superb specimen. I'll enjoy looking at all these of an evening."

He fired a look at his wife to try to tell her not to say any more about his fears. Mrs Brown could not help smiling.

Hunter left and headed towards his own cabin. He paused outside, taking a deep breath before he entered, looking nervously at the portrait of Gonzalo Caboto, as if waiting for it to speak to him.

CHAPTER TEN

A TWINGE IN THE KNEES

Mrs Brown and Paddington both clutched the receiver of a satellite phone while Mr Brown looked on.

Paddington was speaking loudly into the receiver. "I can't talk for long, Mrs Bird. Mr Brown says these satellite phone calls are very expensive."

Back in the Home for Retired Bears, Mrs Bird had the phone in one hand and a paintbrush in the other. She was giving the wall a lick of paint. The Reverend Mother was next to her, looking concerned as she listened in to the phone call.

"The line's breaking up, dear," said Mrs Bird.

"The calls," Paddington repeated, raising his voice. "They're very expensive."

"Pardon?" said Mrs Bird.

"Expensive! E, X, P . . ." Paddington began to spell it out while Mr Brown rolled his eyes and then headed below deck.

The line crackled and a throbbing, humming noise could be heard.

"Ach, it's gone again," said Mrs Bird.

"Well, these satellite phones are very temperamental," said the Reverend Mother.

"It's nae that," said Mrs Bird impatiently. "It's like this building is filled with electrical interference."

"It's just a very old building, Mrs Bird," said the Reverend Mother. "There's nothing suspicious about it."

"Suspicious?" asked Mrs Bird, eyeing the Reverend Mother closely.

The Reverend Mother beamed and silently glided away.

Mrs Bird felt a twinge in her knees. "Oh knees, what are you telling me?" she asked, bobbing up and down.

Suddenly the phone sparked to life again and Mrs Bird snapped back to attention.

It was Mrs Brown, on the boat. "Has there been any sign of Aunt Lucy?" she asked.

"I'm afraid not, no," said Mrs Bird.

Mrs Brown gave Paddington a sympathetic look and put her hand on his arm. "We'll find her, Paddington," she said.

Judy was sitting at the table in her cabin with her headphones on. Mrs Brown came in, clutching the Travel Scrabble set, and started to say something to Judy. She gestured that she couldn't hear, and that Mrs Brown should wait while she took off her headphones.

"Hi, darling," said Mrs Brown. "I was going through my bag and I completely forgot I packed this. Your favourite, isn't it?" She held out the Scrabble set proudly.

Judy barely looked at the board game.

Mrs Brown tried again. "Quick game?"

Judy sighed. "I really need to work on my travelogue."

"*Travelogue*," said Mrs Brown, pointing at the Scrabble set. "Fourteen points, and that's without the triple word score." She beamed.

Judy rolled her eyes and put her headphones back on.

Mrs Brown tried not to look hurt and said to herself, "All right, darling. No, you carry on."

CHAPTER ELEVEN

THE LEGEND OF EL DORADO

It was evening and the boat was moored up for the night. Inside, it was lit up with lots of twinkly lights and a delicious-looking colourful dinner of local vegetables and fruits was laid out for the Browns by their hosts. The family murmured with delight as they took their places at the table.

"*Buen provecho*, my friends," said Hunter, offering a tray of large non-alcoholic cocktails complete with pretty umbrellas. "And to drink, *chicha moradas* – made from Peruvian purple corn. Magenta heaven in a glass." He handed one to Mrs Brown, who was excited to try it.

"Ooo! *¡Muchas gracias!*" she said enthusiastically.

Mr Brown gave her a look.

After handing the drinks out, Hunter said, "Tomorrow we will arrive at Rumi Rock." He held his drink high and gestured to Aunt Lucy's chart on the table. "So, a toast . . ." he announced.

Paddington gave a loud slurp, his snout already inside the glass. He finished the drink off noisily. "Oh, excuse me," he said, looking up at the others. He had a purple juice moustache on his face! He took another drink and held that up for the toast.

"To finding Aunt Lucy . . ." said Hunter.

As everyone raised their drinks, Hunter spotted Aunt Lucy's bracelet on Paddington's arm. He stared at it with a strange intensity.

"Hear, hear!" said Mrs Brown.

Everyone tucked into their drinks. But Hunter's eyes kept darting back to the bracelet. His manner became shifty.

"So, tell me, young bear, why *was* your aunt so interested in Rumi Rock?" he asked.

"We don't know, Mr Hunter," Paddington admitted. "The Reverend Mother said she was looking for something . . ."

"She was wasting her time," said Gina. "Rumi Rock is just a bunch of old stones."

Hunter waited as Gina headed to the galley, then he leaned forward. "A bunch of old stones that, according to legend, is the first step to finding . . . *El Dorado* . . .!"

The Browns all had purple juice moustaches now! They looked up at Hunter with shocked expressions.

Paddington just looked confused. "You mean . . . the piri-piri chicken shop on Edgware Road?"

"He means the mythical lost city," said Jonathan.

"Yes," said Hunter eagerly, "you have all heard the legend of El Dorado? The city made entirely of gold, forever lost in the jungle."

Paddington looked intrigued as Hunter played with a lighter, staring at the flame.

Hunter continued. "You have not heard the true story . . . Would you like to hear it now?" He rested his eyes on Mrs Brown.

"We'd love to!" she said.

"Or after we've eaten," said Mr Brown. "It's probably quite long."

Hunter pulled down a book of old prints from a shelf. In a low voice, he began to explain what they were.

"When the Spanish invaders came, they took all the treasures of Peru – apart from one. The most precious treasure of all – the gold that the Incas valued more than anything else. It could not be found . . ." He turned the page to reveal an image of Incas handing over boxes of golden treasure to some creatures covered with leaves.

Hunter went on: "This is because the Incas had entrusted it to 'Los espíritus del bosque' – the spirits of the forest – who promised to keep it secret and hidden forever." He pointed at the treasure in the pictures and continued. "That is El Dorado."

"Are you suggesting Aunt Lucy was . . . looking for El Dorado?" asked Mrs Brown.

Hunter shrugged. "Aren't we all? In our own ways?"

"No," said Jonathan.

"But why would she be looking for El Dorado, Mrs Brown?" asked Paddington. "She has no interest in gold."

"Let's not get carried away by some old drawings in a book," said Mr Brown. "If El Dorado exists, then why's no one found it?"

"Because none of them had this," said Hunter. He turned another page. It showed a bracelet that looked just like Aunt Lucy's. "It is said," he continued, now staring pointedly at Paddington, "that the only clue the Incas left to where the *espíritus del bosque* hid the gold was in a special bracelet. A bracelet like yours!"

Everyone looked at it, and then looked at the bracelet on Paddington's arm.

"Where did you get that?" asked Gina.

"It's Aunt Lucy's," said Paddington. "She always wore it."

"It is the key to finding El Dorado!" cried Hunter. He grabbed Paddington and pulled the bracelet into the light.

"Wow!" said Mrs Brown.

"There's no reason why Aunt Lucy would have an ancient Inca bracelet," said Mr Brown.

"But she did!" said Judy. "Look! It's the same!" She pulled Paddington's paw as well.

"It may well look the same . . ." began Mr Brown.

"Honestly, Henry," said Mrs Brown, "you're really taking the fun out of this."

Paddington's paw was being yanked around the table as everyone discussed the bracelet.

"It's just an ordinary stringy bracelet," said Mr Brown, but he grabbed Paddington's paw too.

"It is not an ordinary bracelet," said Hunter. "It is quipu."

"Quip-who?" said Mr Brown.

Hunter whipped the bracelet off and poor Paddington immediately fell over. Hunter stretched out the bracelet so that everyone could see it was made with a complex set of colourful knots. "An ancient Inca knot language used for secret messages," he said, pointing at each in turn, "hidden in riddles . . ."

Mr Brown rolled his eyes.

Paddington stared at the bracelet. "So, if we work out what this says, it might help us find Aunt Lucy?" he asked.

"I believe so," said Hunter, "and maybe even find El Dorado itself!"

Mr Brown looked doubtful. "I'm sorry, but I don't buy it. It's just some drawings in a book, a mysterious bracelet, and a secret Inca riddle that . . ." He paused, realising what he was saying. "I suppose it *is* starting to stack up."

"Lend me this bracelet for a few hours," said Hunter. "I may be able to translate it."

Gina gave her father a sharp look. "Everyone who searches for El Dorado dies," she said.

There was a wave of silence as this sank in.

"Then we can't let that happen to Aunt Lucy," said Paddington firmly. He handed the bracelet to Hunter.

CHAPTER TWELVE

THE GHOST
OF CABOTO

The Browns were getting ready for bed. Judy was on the top bunk in the cabin she shared with Jonathan. She was flicking through Mr Gruber's travel book. She paused at the picture of Gonzalo Caboto . . . then sniffed the air in disgust. "What is that smell?" she asked.

On the bottom bunk Jonathan had been spraying Teenage Boy deodorant on himself. "Gotta smell good in the jungle, you know," he said.

Mrs Brown called out from the cabin she was sharing with Mr Brown. "Night, night!"

Jonathan called back, "Night."

Mrs Brown was in bed sketching a drawing of Aunt Lucy. "Love you!" she called out. She waited hopefully but no response came. Mr Brown popped up from under the bed, wearing a head torch.

"Clear!" he announced.

Mrs Brown ignored him. "Very interesting man, Hunter, isn't he?" she said absently.

"Right," said Mr Brown, sounding fed up.

"If what he says is true," Mrs Brown went on, "we could be on our way to finding Aunt Lucy *and* the lost city of El Dorado!"

"I hope so, for Paddington's sake," said Mr Brown. "But, in my experience, tattooed charmers can't always be relied upon."

Paddington meanwhile was out on the deck, trying to clamber into his hammock. He jumped in and was immediately spun out of it, his arms and legs flailing in all directions. He kept trying to get into it, talking to it in the hope it would stop moving.

"Nice hammock! Steady, steady!" he said.

In the final cabin, Hunter was wide awake. He was studying Aunt Lucy's bracelet with a magnifying glass, making notes on a piece of paper and trying to decode the ancient message hidden in the knots. He was not alone.

The ghost of Hunter's gold-hunter ancestor, Gonzalo Caboto, had appeared from the portrait and was pacing behind him impatiently. "What does it say?" he demanded.

"It doesn't make any sense," said Hunter.

"Why not?" asked Caboto angrily.

"Because it's a riddle!"

Suddenly Gina appeared at his doorway, looking suspicious. "Who are you talking to?" she asked. She couldn't see or hear the ghost of Caboto.

"No one," lied Hunter.

"You're seeing the ghosts again, aren't you?" said Gina. She looked worried. "We need to turn back!"

"Gina, I'm fine," said Hunter. He grinned broadly to show everything was all right.

Gina was not convinced. "You made me a promise," she said. "We don't need gold."

"You're right," Hunter agreed wholeheartedly. "But if we had it," he went on in a persuasive tone, "we could buy a real house with stairs and beds and . . . square windows!"

"Papa!" Gina exclaimed.

"We could bring honour to the family," said Hunter.

"But we only need each other," Gina insisted. She looked really worried now. "You've got that look in your eye. I'm scared I'm going to lose you again – for good this time. Please, turn the boat round, Papa."

Hunter looked at the ghost of Caboto and then looked at the quipu on the table.

"Do not listen to her!" hissed Caboto. "She does not understand – we need the gold! THE GLORY!"

"You're right . . ." said Hunter. He slipped the bracelet into his pocket and leaped up. "Let's turn the boat right round, Gina," he said. "Right now."

"You mean it?" said Gina.

"You're my treasure, and I love you," he said.

"Thank you," said Gina, relieved.

Caboto looked very angry, but Hunter ignored him. "Go and untie the mooring rope," he told his daughter.

Gina went out on to the riverbank in the warm night air. She was busy untying the rope, with her back to the boat. "I'm so proud of you, Papa. This could be a whole new chapter in our . . ." She pulled her end of the rope free . . . then realised the other end had been cut! She whipped round to see the boat drifting off, leaving her stranded on the riverbank.

"PAPA!"

Hunter stood on the boat, waving, with Caboto standing next to him.

"I love you, Gina, but I have to get that gold. I have to! I'm doing this for the both of us . . .!"

Caboto nodded sympathetically.

Gina ran down the bank. "You double-crossing pig . . . *¡Maldito! ¡Estúpido! ¡Escoria!*"

"What a potty mouth," said Caboto. Then he said to Hunter cheerfully, "And you – you really had me there! Maybe you're not a failure after all." He became serious again. "Come, we've got work to do."

Hunter hesitated, watching as the current took him away from his daughter. He felt terrible that he had tricked Gina, but he wanted that gold so much . . . He turned away and followed Caboto just as the boat hit some rapids and bounced a little. There was an ominous CREAK and a long shadow swung towards Hunter.

"What's that creaking noise?" Caboto asked.

Hunter realised too late. "Boom!" he shouted.

THWACK! The boom hit him hard and knocked him overboard into the dark water.

SPLASH!

Caboto immediately vanished.

CHAPTER THIRTEEN

TROUBLE ABOARD!

Paddington was asleep, tangled up in his hammock, clutching Aunt Lucy's glasses. Drops of water landed on him from above. He twitched a bit in his sleep and wiped his face and then began dreaming of Mr Gruber's statue before he was blinded by mystical golden light . . .

Paddington awoke with a gasp and fell out of his hammock. "Oof!" he cried, looking around and shielding his eyes from the morning sun. His dream had left him feeling troubled.

As the boat chugged on upriver, the Browns came up on the dining deck at the stern. They cheerfully took their places at the table.

"I spy, with my little eye, something beginning with 'J'," said Mrs Brown.

"Is it 'jungle'?" asked Jonathan.

"No, it's something else . . ." said Mrs Brown.

Paddington arrived, still clutching Aunt Lucy's glasses.

"Sleep well, Paddington?" Mrs Brown asked.

"I keep having the strangest dream," said Paddington. "Has anyone seen Mr Hunter? I'd love to know if he's translated the bracelet . . ."

"Or at least made us some breakfast," said Mr Brown.

Mrs Brown gave him a piercing look.

"Well, it's gone past ten, Mary!" said Mr Brown indignantly. He looked around and called out, "Hello? Any chance of some coffee?"

Paddington went down the ladder to the saloon to see if he could find Gina or her father. It was eerily empty below deck.

He called out, "Coo-ee! Mr Hunter?" Then he paused before the portraits of Hunter's ancestors. They seemed to be glaring at him. He lifted his hat politely. Suddenly the boat

bumped a little, jolting the piano, making it
start playing automatically. Paddington leaped
in shock, stumbling backwards into the globe
drinks cabinet, which he suddenly found
himself sitting inside, among the various bottles.
The globe trundled backwards and clonked
against a shelf. The impact sent a jar rolling.
Paddington gasped in horror as he realised it
was marmalade.

"NO . . .!" He popped Aunt Lucy's glasses
down on the counter and leaped to catch the
falling jar. He managed to catch it and let out a
sigh of relief. "Phew . . .!" He was about to put
the marmalade back, but paused for a moment,
gazing at the delicious treat . . .

Moments later, Paddington stepped up into the
wheelhouse, guiltily wiping his mouth and
holding an empty marmalade jar.

"Um, Gina," he began, "we seem to have
run out of marmala . . ." but then he stopped –
there was NOBODY AT THE WHEEL!

Paddington thought for a moment, then
spotted the dangling microphone. He quickly

clambered up the spokes of the ship's wheel
and grabbed it, but doing this made the wheel
spin round and the boat lurched dangerously to
the side.

Outside on the dining deck, Mr Brown said,
"Is it me or is it getting a bit choppy?" Then
he had an idea. "Actually, Judy – take another
photo!" He put on his sunglasses again as Judy
snapped a shot of him trying to lean in a cool
way on the boat rail.

Above deck in the wheelhouse, Paddington
was now hanging above the ship's wheel,
tangled up in the curly microphone cable. The
boat lurched again, and his hat fell off.

Back on the dining deck, the speaker
crackled to life. It was Paddington's voice on
the ship's loudspeaker!

"Er . . . good morning. Could the Brown
family pop up to the front of the boat for an
. . . um . . . emergency?"

The Browns looked at each other. Then they
leaped into action.

* * *

Up ahead, the river divided into two. The boat was now veering away from the main branch of the river into a smaller stream, churning with white rapids. There were lots of large rocks in the water, which made the boat tip from side to side so that, on board, the Browns were sent flying! They staggered through the saloon towards the wheelhouse as the boat heaved violently. However, just as they reached the entrance, the piano, still playing a jolly tune, broke loose from its fixings and rolled in front of them, blocking their path. They yelled to Paddington through the wheelhouse doorway.

"Paddington, what on earth are you doing in there?" Mrs Brown shouted.

Paddington, still tangled in microphone cable, was now attempting to steer the boat away from danger with his feet. The boat leaned again, and a captain's hat dropped on to his head.

"Um . . . I appear to be driving the boat, Mrs Brown," he said.

"What? Where's Gina?" asked Mr Brown.

"She's not here!" said Paddington. "I don't think Mr Hunter's here either!"

"DAD!" Judy shouted. Through the window, she had spotted bigger rapids ahead.

"Paddington, put it in reverse," cried Mr Brown. "Put the boat in reverse!"

"Good idea!" said Paddington. "Hmm . . . reverse . . ." He spotted a large lever and pulled it down with his foot. There was a loud noise from the engines and the propellers churned as the boat accelerated forward. "Oh no . . . that's faster!" cried Paddington.

Inside, the sudden speed of the boat made the Browns tumble back into the saloon, swiftly followed by the piano.

Paddington, meanwhile, had clutched on to the ship's wheel, which suddenly came off in his paws.

The piano was now playing a jolly tune that was like a soundtrack for a chase! The Browns leaped through the back door just in time to avoid the piano jamming into the doorway. They collapsed in a heap – right back where they had started. It was then that Mr Brown spotted the mooring rope, hanging free.

"We've got to stop the engine!" said
Jonathan.

"Where are the life jackets?" asked Judy.

"Over there!" said Mrs Brown.

Mr Brown and Jonathan ran up one side of
the boat, Mrs Brown and Judy ran up the
other. As they passed the wheelhouse, Judy
peered through the window.

"Where's Paddington?" she cried.

The wheelhouse was now empty . . . and the
ship's wheel had also disappeared . . .

CHAPTER FOURTEEN

"ABANDON SHIP!"

Meanwhile, back in the wheelhouse, Mrs Brown had found a hatch labelled "Emergency Supplies". She yanked it open to find it was full of cocktail shakers, drinks and tiny umbrellas, which were no use at all!

Jonathan and Mr Brown were running along the side of the deck as the boat tossed and heaved in the angry white water, the hull crashing against huge boulders. They stopped in their tracks when they saw Paddington, who had accidentally become lashed to the ship's wheel by the microphone cable! Mr Brown and Jonathan whirled round to go in the opposite direction as Paddington rolled towards them at a dangerous speed. The boat then suddenly lurched, causing Paddington to roll away from them. Mr Brown and Jonathan chased after him. Then the ship's wheel collided with some steps and smashed, sending Paddington flying towards the bow!

Paddington landed in a heap in front of Mrs Brown and Judy. He sat up, dazed, still holding two handles of the ship's wheel, but realised the rest of it had disappeared. He had at least found the life jackets, when his fall on the bow broke open their locker.

"Er . . . abandon ship?" Paddington suggested.

"Yes!" shouted Mrs Brown. "ABANDON SHIP!"

The Browns gathered by the rail in their life jackets, and then everyone leaped into the water except Paddington.

He gasped in horror as he remembered something. "Aunt Lucy's glasses!" he cried, and rushed back down into the boat.

Seconds later, Paddington stumbled into the

saloon. The boat was rolling violently now, and water was spouting from all directions. Just then, Paddington spotted Aunt Lucy's glasses sliding around on the counter where he had left them. He was about to reach them when the whole room started turning round and round like a spinning barrel! Paddington had to run on the spot to stay upright, like a hamster in a wheel, as he stretched for Aunt Lucy's glasses.

Out in the water, beyond the rapids, the Browns were bobbing in the water, spluttering and coughing.

"Grab anything that floats!" shouted Mr Brown. Taking his own advice, he snatched at something, only to find it was the case containing the purple-kneed tarantula!

"ARRGH! It's that spider again!" He pushed it away, then saw his risk manual floating past and threw his arms round it. He muttered gratefully to himself, "Triple-laminated . . ."

"Wait," said Mrs Brown, looking around. "Where's Paddington? Paddington!"

Just as the Browns were starting to panic, a

circle of bubbles appeared as if something large
was about to surface.

SPLOOOSH! Paddington burst out of
the water. He was now sitting on top of the
piano, which was still playing a gurgling
version of its jaunty tune!

"I'm here! I'm okay, everyone!" he cried. He
held up Aunt Lucy's glasses triumphantly.
"Aunt Lucy's going to need these."

Soon the Browns and Paddington reached the
shore and pulled themselves up on to the bank.
Everyone was completely soaked through.

Mrs Brown took in their surroundings.
"Where are we?" she asked.

"The Amazon," said Jonathan.

"Brilliant," said Mr Brown sarcastically.

Judy reached into her soggy clothes. She
pulled out her Dictaphone, shook the water out
of it and turned it on to start recording some
more of her travelogue. "Day three. With the
Browns lost in the jungle, everyone was
thinking the same thing. How long till we eat
each other?"

Mr Brown gave his daughter a stern look and said, "That's not helpful, Judy."

Bits and pieces from the boat floated past them, including the satellite phone. It was ringing as it sank into the river . . .

. . . Mrs Bird was phoning them from the Home for Retired Bears. She listened as the ringtone crackled, then went dead.

Mrs Bird looked at the receiver, puzzled. "What's wrong with this thing?"

She jiggled the phone cable in the socket, then noticed something on the wall behind the desk. There was a curious electrical junction box up there, which had a high voltage sign on it. Mrs Bird realised that there was a throbbing, humming noise coming from it. A large red industrial electrical cable ran out of the box and along the wall.

"What have we here . . .?" she said to herself.

Mrs Bird quickly followed the mysterious red cable around the Home for Retired Bears. It travelled under rugs, around a bear's rocking chair, between the legs of a statue of the Virgin Mary . . .

"Pardon me," she said as she reached under the statue.

She followed the cable past a nun who was calling out bingo numbers and got momentarily distracted.

"Noah's Ark – all the 2s," called out the bingo nun, holding up the number 22. "Days and Nights 40, Days and Nights. All the Apostles, number 12. The Holy Trinity, number 3. Three Wise Men, number 3. The Commandments, number 10. Genesis, number 1. All the Horsemen, number 4! Horseman of the Apocalypse, number 4. 67, Stairway to Heaven. 33, Part the Sea. 52, God bless you. Pieces of Silver, 30."

Mrs Bird shook her head and concentrated on following the cable until it disappeared into the wall next to an elaborate church organ. There was a gap in the wall round the organ, and from inside the gap came a strange red glow that throbbed in time with the humming noise. The noise seemed to be coming from behind the wall! Mrs Bird was inspecting the organ when the Reverend Mother quietly appeared as if from nowhere.

"Do you play, Mrs Bird?" she asked, a calm smile playing on her lips.

Mrs Bird ignored her question. "What's behind that organ?" she demanded.

"Nothing to be concerned about," said the Reverend Mother.

"What about the lights?" Mrs Bird persisted. "And the humming?"

"It's just a secret room," said the Reverend Mother.

"Secret room?" Mrs Bird gasped. "What have you got in there?"

"I'm afraid I can't tell you," said the Reverend Mother.

Mrs Bird frowned. "That's strange. And why is that?"

"I don't know what you're finding strange, Mrs Bird," said the Reverend Mother, looking puzzled. "It's just a secret room, behind an organ, and I can't tell you what's in it. There's nothing suspicious about it."

"That's the second time you've used the word 'suspicious'!" said Mrs Bird.

"Oh, is it?" The Reverend Mother beamed the same radiant smile. "Well, the Lord moves in suspicious ways."

"Don't you mean *mysterious* ways?" said Mrs Bird.

The Reverend Mother looked surprised. "You know your scripture, Mrs Bird! Now come along – it's time for bingo." And, with that, she led an unconvinced Mrs Bird away from the organ.

"Aye . . . bingo!" said Mrs Bird decisively.

CHAPTER FIFTEEN

LOST . . .

Paddington and the bedraggled Browns stood on the riverbank, surveying the debris from the boat wreck.

"Well . . . we wanted a holiday to remember!" said Mrs Brown, trying to sound cheerful.

"At this rate, we might not be around to remember it," said Mr Brown grumpily.

"Maybe we should just, like, draw a big SOS in the sand and chill here?" said Jonathan.

"'Chill here'?" Mr Brown repeated, disgusted. "This is the Amazon, not a shopping centre!"

"All we need is a plan," said Mrs Brown.

"I have a plan, Mrs Brown," said Paddington.
Everyone turned to look at him in surprise.

"We find Rumi Rock ourselves." Paddington
wrung out his wet hat and placed it decisively
on his head. "It can't be far – and whatever's
happened to Hunter and Gina, they're bound
to look for us there."

"Are you *sure* you can find the way?" asked
Mrs Brown.

"The jungle was my home, Mrs Brown,"
said Paddington firmly. "I think I know my
way around."

Mr Brown glanced down at Paddington's
umbrella, which had survived the wreckage.
"But . . . you have spent rather a long time in
London, Paddington."

Paddington put his foot up on a log and
leaned on his knee, giving Mr Brown a steely
look. "Mr Brown. You can take the bear out
of the jungle, but you can't take the jungle
out of the bear."

The log started moving and let out a low
growl. An alarmed Paddington yelped and
quickly pulled his foot away as it revealed

itself to be something large and reptilian, which slithered into the undergrowth.

"Ahem, anyway . . . follow me," said Paddington hastily. "Oh, and remember, whatever you do, never touch this plant." He pointed at a very spiky bright red plant.

"What's it called?" Judy asked.

"The Spiky Red One," Paddington announced confidently. He strode off into the undergrowth, followed tentatively by the Browns. "A short stroll in the jungle," he said over his shoulder. "This'll be fun!"

The Browns followed Paddington through the trees.

"This way! Rumi Rock should be just through . . . here!" Paddington announced.

They walked on, pushing through the dense leaves and branches, until they reached another part of the rainforest.

". . . through . . . here . . ." repeated Paddington.

By now, the Browns were covered in dirt and twigs.

They made their way towards a large waterfall, surrounded by closely packed trees. They leaped across the water using stepping stones.

"THROUGH . . ." Paddington shouted above the noise of the waterfall, "HERE . . ."

After hours of trekking, the Browns were feeling very weary.

"Paddington . . . are you sure you know where you're going?" Mr Brown asked anxiously.

"Oh yes, Mr Brown," said Paddington. "When you're from the jungle, you don't miss a thing. Like this! Look!" He pointed at a leaf.

"A . . . leaf?" asked Mr Brown, puzzled.

"No. A leaf insect," said Paddington. The leaf insect started to move. "You see, Mr Brown? I don't miss a thing."

The Browns were impressed and reassured. Paddington walked off confidently. Behind them, some large figures made entirely of leaves stepped out unnoticed from their perfectly camouflaged hiding place in the undergrowth.

These were the *espíritus del bosque*, who silently began to follow the Browns and Paddington through the rainforest.

After miles and miles of walking through more and more vegetation and enormous trees, Paddington pushed through a bush and announced, "And if I'm not mistaken, Rumi Rock will be right through . . . oh . . ."

He stopped and stared.

They were back at the riverbank with the boat wreck! Their footprints were still in the sand at the exact spot where they had started their trek.

"Marvellous." Mr Brown sounded very fed up.

Paddington dropped his head in shame. "Mr Brown was right. Maybe I have spent too long in London."

"It's okay, Paddington." Mrs Brown put a comforting hand on him.

Paddington looked at her, full of despair as the rain started to fall. "Only a spot of drizzle," he said, trying to sound brave. But the drizzle

quickly became very heavy rain indeed and
soon everyone was drenched.

Miserably, the Browns pulled their clothes
tighter around them.

"How long will it rain like this?" Judy asked.

Paddington looked up into the darkening sky.
"Could be a few minutes . . . or a few months."

The Browns looked at each other uncertainly.

"Let's find some shelter for the night," said
Mrs Brown.

CHAPTER SIXTEEN
RUMI ROCK

The rain was still falling heavily. The Browns had taken up residence in the roots of a giant kapok tree. Jonathan looked up at a tasty-looking fruit on a low-hanging branch. It made him think of one of his inventions. *That branch could be the extendable arm of a newly made Snack Hack*, he thought to himself. *I could make it from twigs and vines. Then the branch could knock the fruit to the floor so that I could reach it . . .* Jonathan sighed. Would he ever get home to his real Snack Hack?

"I spy with my little eye," said Mrs Brown, "something beginning with . . ." Then she heard a distant screech that made her jump. "Doesn't matter," she said hastily.

"Let's do our best to get some sleep," Mr Brown suggested.

"Night night, Paddington," said Mrs Brown. "We'll try again in the morning."

"Night night. Sleep tight. Don't let the giant tree bugs bite," replied Paddington.

"Giant tree bugs . . .?" Mr Brown repeated nervously.

But Paddington wasn't listening to him. He was already climbing higher up the tree trunk, looking for a comfy "attic" branch on which to settle. The voices of the Browns gave way to the sounds of the forest as he climbed higher.

A few branches below, Judy was recording her travelogue again. "End of day three. Faint from cold and hunger, soaked to the skin, we're forced to take shelter in a bug-infested kapok tree . . ."

"Please, Judy. Not now," said Mr Brown.

"Tempers are getting frayed," Judy continued.

"They are NOT getting frayed," said Mr Brown.

". . . said my father," Judy went on. "His temper fraying."

"Well, I'm sorry," Mr Brown snapped. "I'm sleeping in a tree. I've got wet socks! I can practically *hear* the spiders!"

"What happened to 'embracing the risk'?" asked Mrs Brown.

"I've tried that, Mary! God knows I've tried!" cried Mr Brown in exasperation. "But I've been living a lie! I'm Henry Brown and I'm risk averse. I don't belong here, we don't belong here and, frankly, neither does Paddington any more."

Paddington had reached the top of the tree. He pushed his head up through the leaves and emerged above the canopy. The endless jungle stretched out in every direction. He had heard what Mr Brown had said and now the enormity of his task was sinking in. He sighed, feeling hope seep away from him for the first time since they had left the Home for Retired Bears. Above him, grey clouds gathered in the night sky, and more and more tropical rain poured down on him. Paddington pulled out his Windsorman Deluxe umbrella, which he had been carrying with him all the way. He popped it open and huddled beneath it.

"Where *are* you, Aunt Lucy?" he said, staring longingly out into the forest.

Eventually Paddington drifted off to sleep and fell into a dream. It was broad daylight in the dream, and Paddington was walking along a rope-bridge towards the door of the old treehouse in which he'd grown up. He peered through the doorway and was surprised to see Aunt Lucy sitting in her rocking chair.

"Aunt Lucy – I thought I'd lost you!" cried Paddington.

"Oh, Paddington," said Aunt Lucy gently. "Can't you see that it is you who are lost?"

Paddington cried out, "Aunt Lucy!"

Then he woke with a gasp. He was back in the tree, soaking wet, mouthing silently, "Aunt Lucy!"

He looked for his umbrella, but it had been
blown from his grasp into the next tree.
Paddington clambered after it, but somehow
the umbrella was always just beyond his reach.
He chased it down through the trees. At times,
it looked as if the trees had taken hold of the
umbrella and were passing it on to one
another using their leafy branches as though
they were hands.

Paddington clambered down to the floor of
the forest, racing after his umbrella, but it was
always just ahead of him, seeming to blow
away on the breeze. He ran on and on until
he lost his footing and tumbled down the
bank. There was a huge SPLASH! Paddington
fell into the umbrella, which was now
upended and acting as a little boat! It carried
Paddington along on the current.

After a while Paddington spotted some
bushes ahead of him on the far bank. They
were gently drawing apart like a pair of
curtains. What was going on in there?
Paddington decided to find out. He saw a
branch floating ahead of him and plucked it

from the water. Using the branch as a paddle, he made his way towards the gap in the bushes. It was hard work, paddling against the rushing river, but eventually he reached the opposite bank.

He climbed out of the water, taking his umbrella with him, and made his way into the jungle. The rainforest was becoming denser and darker, and Paddington was beginning to wonder if he should turn back. But he had come this far. He told himself to be brave and pushed on through the darkness, even though he could barely see a thing.

Just as he was thinking how hopeless this was, he reached a clearing. He stopped for a moment to catch his breath . . . then there was a crash of thunder and a bright flash of lightning! Paddington threw up his paws and almost toppled over from shock! But then, in the flash of light, he saw something incredible: a towering statue of a bear! It was just like the one Paddington had seen in Mr Gruber's shop, only massive and made of stone. It looked like the one from his dream in the hammock . . .

Paddington was completely confused. In his mind he was back in Mr Gruber's shop for a moment, staring at the statue . . . Then just as quickly he was back in the jungle again. He could see now that the clearing was encircled by ancient stones and the bear statue was right in the centre. And there was Hunter, looking as stylish as ever – except for the fact that his neatly buttoned suit was now absolutely filthy.

"Ah. Little bear. I was wondering when you'd turn up," said Hunter.

"Mr Hunter! Thank goodness you're safe!" said Paddington.

Hunter gestured to the stone circle. "Welcome to Rumi Rock."

"And Aunt Lucy – is she here?" Paddington looked around hopefully.

"No," said Hunter. "But I think she *was* here. Remember I told you Rumi Rock was the gateway to El Dorado? That's why no one can find her here, Paddington, because she's already found her way there."

"Why do you think that, Mr Hunter?" Paddington asked.

Hunter revealed the bracelet and smiled.

"You translated the quipu!" Paddington exclaimed. "What does it say?"

"It says . . ."

Paddington's eyes widened in anticipation.

"'At Rumi Rock, the bear will show the way.'" Hunter handed the bracelet back to Paddington.

Paddington's eyes widened still further, then he suddenly looked blank.

"And what bear would that be?" he asked.

"You tell me. You're the bear," said Hunter, raising an eyebrow.

"I see," said Paddington, frowning. "And does the bracelet say anything else at all?"

"Just 'The bear will show the way'," said Hunter, getting more annoyed by the minute.

"I see. And there isn't another message, written on the back? Because sometimes . . ."

"NO!" Hunter snapped. "It says, 'The bear will show the way.' You're a bear, that's a bear, that talisman's got a bear on it. This whole thing's really BEARY! So what do we do – *BEAR*?" he asked pointedly.

"I don't know, Mr Hunter," said Paddington. "Aunt Lucy always says, 'When you're faced with a problem, sit down and put on your thinking cap.'" Paddington put his hat on his head and sat down to think hard.

Unfortunately, he had sat right on the spiky red plant. Paddington leaped up, clutching his bottom. He opened his mouth and let out a mighty roar of pain.

"ROARRRRRRRRRGHHHHHHHH!"

The roar bounced around the stone circle and became louder and louder. The force of the roar sent a shockwave through the jungle. Birds burst out of the trees, cawing loudly.

The shockwave even reached the sleeping Browns. Jonathan's fringe was blown into the air. He sleepily patted it back down again. The exhausted family stirred, but didn't wake up.

Back at Rumi Rock, Hunter was taken aback by the roar. Indeed, Paddington seemed to have shocked himself.

He looked down at the plant and tutted. "Please excuse me, Mr Hunter. It seems I sat on the Spiky Red One."

And then the strangest thing happened. They heard, very faintly in the distance, someone roaring back!

"What was that?" Hunter asked, shocked.

Paddington looked ahead dreamily and repeated Aunt Lucy's words to himself in a whisper: "'If you ever get lost again, just roar and I'll roar right back.'"

He stepped into the middle of the circle and roared again. The roar echoed around the jungle. Paddington waited and listened. Then there was another even louder reply.

Paddington gasped. "Aunt Lucy! She can hear me! Aunt Lucy!" Paddington roared again.

And the roar replied!

"That's how we find her, Mr Hunter," said Paddington excitedly. "Like she always said. Follow her roars!"

Suddenly the ghost of Gonzalo Caboto the gold hunter appeared to Hunter, smiling darkly. "The bear shows the way," he muttered.

"Yes!" said Hunter. "We follow the roars, and the gold will be OURS! *Yours*, your aunt's . . ." He hurriedly corrected himself, smiling at

Paddington. "We'll find your Aunt Gold. I mean . . . Aunt Lucy! Let's go!"

There was a sudden crash of thunder, and Hunter was saved from Paddington seeing just how guilty he looked as they rushed into the jungle . . .

CHAPTER SEVENTEEN
THE SECRET ROOM

The thunder could be heard all the way over on the other side of the jungle in the Home for Retired Bears. The Reverend Mother poked her head round the door to Mrs Bird's cabin to check on her. It seemed that she was soundly asleep in her bed, undisturbed by the thunder. However, the moment the Reverend Mother left, Mrs Bird's eyes opened – she had been faking all along!

"Come on, knees," said Mrs Bird, "let's get to the bottom of this!" She jumped up and slipped out of the bedroom, silently following

the Reverend Mother as she hurried through
the cloisters.

The Reverend Mother disappeared round a
corner. Mrs Bird followed . . . but the
Reverend Mother was nowhere to be seen!
There was only the organ, which was glowing
all around its edges with a strange red light.
Mrs Bird approached it and noticed one of the
buttons was more worn than the others. She
pulled it and the entire organ flipped round
like a revolving door, taking Mrs Bird into
. . . a secret room! It looked like somewhere a
spy might hide – there were maps all over the
walls, lots of computer screens and red lights
flashing everywhere.

"What in God's name . . .?" cried Mrs Bird.

The Reverend Mother suddenly turned in
her seat. "Language, Mrs Bird!" she scolded.

"Pardon me, Reverend Mother," said Mrs
Bird. "But this place . . . it . . . kind of looks
like an evil lair."

"I can assure you it's not."

"Then what is it?" asked Mrs Bird.

"What it is, is a . . . perfectly innocent secret

surveillance control centre," said the Reverend Mother hurriedly.

Mrs Bird narrowed her eyes. "And why exactly would you need one of those?" she asked.

The Reverend Mother wrung her hands. "I confess! I have sinned, Mrs Bird! I have been deceitful, in a way most unbecoming of a nun! I can only pray for your forgiveness!"

"What have you done . . .?" asked Mrs Bird, astonished.

"The St Christopher medallion I gave Mary – it . . . was actually a secret tracking device." The Reverend Mother flicked some switches on a control panel. "I couldn't let what happened to poor Aunt Lucy ever happen again . . . so I've been keeping an eye on them."

She pressed a button and a map on the wall lit up with bleeping lights.

"This is a canny bit of kit!" said Mrs Bird in wonder. "Someone's been a busy nun."

"Thank goodness I have," said the Reverend Mother. "Look . . ." She pointed to the map. "This is Rumi Rock, and this is the

Browns' course. They were heading the right way – but now, they've turned north into uncharted, dangerous jungle . . . and I fear for their safety."

Mrs Bird reached for a phone. "I'll notify the authorities. We'll mount a rescue party!"

The Reverend Mother put her hand over Mrs Bird's. "No!" she shouted, then quickly pulled herself together. "They will be too slow. We must go ourselves," she said more calmly.

"But I thought you didnae go trekking in the jungle? Thought it gave ye the heebie-jeebies?" said Mrs Bird.

"Oh, I wasn't planning on trekking . . ." said the Reverend Mother. She held up a set of keys and shook them.

Mrs Bird looked intrigued.

In the jungle the next morning, Mr Brown was sleeping blissfully among the roots of a giant kapok tree. He was so fast asleep, that when *someone* started nuzzling and licking his face he thought it was Mrs Brown trying to wake him with a morning kiss!

"Mmm, Mary . . . not with the kids around—" He opened his eyes and saw that he was face to face with an anteater.

It squealed.

Mr Brown shrieked.

The anteater charged off into the jungle!

"Shhhh!" said Mrs Brown. She looked up, her finger to her lips, and pointed into the undergrowth. "There's something big out there . . ."

Something was crashing towards them. Mrs Brown slowly reached down to the forest floor and groped around for something she might be able to use as a weapon.

"Hello . . .?" she called out. "Whatever you are, you should know I've got a –" she glanced at what she was holding – "a . . . twig . . . and I'm not afraid to use it." She tried to sound brave.

"It could be the forest spirits!" said Judy nervously.

The bushes immediately burst into life! The family jolted in shock, and Mrs Brown ran into the bushes with a war cry.

"YAAAAAAAARRRRHHHH!"

The bushes thrashed about and there was a loud BONK! followed by an "OW".

"Oh my gosh," Mrs Brown said politely. "I'm SO sorry. My mistake," and retreated apologetically.

It was Gina! She emerged, rubbing her head. "*¡Hola*, Browns!" She made the sign of the cross on her chest and added gratefully, "*¡Gracias a Dios!* You're okay."

"Pretty pleased to see you too," said Mr Brown, relieved. He joined the children. Jonathan realised his hair was sticking up and quickly patted it back down as they all gathered around Gina.

"It was very clever to use Jonathan's insect repellent as an odour trail," said Gina.

"Oh, yeah, I mean . . . that was the idea," said Jonathan, trying to sound impressive.

Judy shot him a knowing glance.

"Where on earth did you go?" asked Mr Brown. "You and your father abandoned us. On a ship! Which we had to abandon!"

"Yes . . . my father," said Gina, pulling a face.

"I'm afraid there is something about him . . . about us . . . that I should have told you from the very beginning." She sank on to a log, looking troubled. The Browns waited for her to continue, intrigued. "My family is cursed with a dreadful disease," she said. "They call it *oro loco* – gold madness. A lust for gold that cannot be satisfied. It began with my ancestor Gonzalo Caboto . . ."

"The famous conquistador," said Judy. "*That's* why he seemed familiar!"

"Gonzalo was greedy and ruthless. And when he heard the legend of El Dorado he came looking for it in the jungle, searching endlessly, driving his men to exhaustion. But it was pointless. Instead of riches, all he passed on to his descendants was greed. Generation after generation of fools, obsessed by their pursuit of El Dorado. The Cabot family gold hunters travelled from every corner of the globe." She began counting off on her fingers: "There was the Edwardian explorer, Colonel Clive Cabeaufort; the gold prospector, Calamity Caboot; the Swedish airwoman, Cagnetta

Cabot-Cabotstrom and the missionary, Reverend Cuthbert McCabotty. They came from all walks of life, but all any of them found was death.

"My father was different. Mama died when I was young so it was always just us. He was determined to beat the family curse. But when he heard of Rumi Rock it took hold of him. He disappeared into the jungle and I was left alone . . . for years. When he returned a broken man, he promised he would keep away from the jungle and its ghosts. He would stick to the river and never love gold more than me. And I believed him . . . Seems I was a fool."

"Oh, Gina . . ." Mrs Brown said sadly. Then she noticed Mr Brown shrugging. "What is it?"

"Nothing," said Mr Brown innocently. "Just goes to show you should never trust a handsome river captain."

"I never said he was handsome," said Mrs Brown.

"You were thinking it!" said Mr Brown indignantly.

"Now *oro loco* has taken him," Gina went

on, ignoring Mr Brown, "he is haunted by the ghosts of ancestors and will do anything to find the gold. I *must* get you and Paddington to safety," she said firmly.

"Hang on, where *is* Paddington?" Jonathan asked, looking around.

The Browns exchanged anxious glances. No one had seen Paddington for hours!

CHAPTER EIGHTEEN

FOLLOWING ROARS

Paddington was, in fact, making his way through the jungle, roaring loudly!

"RRRROOOARRRR!"

He was up a tree, striking a confident pose as he roared into the mountain air. After a short pause there was a faint ROAR back!

Hunter was behind Paddington, crossing a rope bridge over a wide river. In the distance he could hear Paddington calling, "THIS WAY, MR HUNTER!"

Hunter yelled back. "I'LL BE RIGHT WITH YOU!" But he held up his machete and was just about to cut the bridge . . .! Then he stopped, as though having second thoughts, but the ghost of Caboto urged him on.

"That's right! Don't let them follow us!" Caboto encouraged him.

"But we won't be able to go back . . ." Hunter argued.

"WE CAN BUY OUR WAY BACK!" Caboto cried.

Hunter nodded and hacked down the supports of the rope bridge. They collapsed into the water and started to sink. Then, grim-faced, he set off in Paddington's direction.

A little while later, Hunter and Paddington were resting by a newly lit fire. Hunter was boiling some drinking water. Paddington was expertly tearing open some jungle fruit, slurping out the good bits and discarding the husks. He started speaking with his mouth full.

"And you're sure the River Taxi Service will have rescued the Browns by now, Mr Hunter?" asked Paddington.

"Yes, of course," said Hunter shiftily, not quite meeting Paddington's eyes.

"Oh, that's good. Mr Brown did have some rather wet socks!" said Paddington, spitting out another bit of husk. "We're getting close now, Mr Hunter. I can feel it! One more push and we'll be with Aunt Lucy!"

"And all the gold of El Dorado!" muttered Hunter.

"Oh yes, I'd forgotten about all that," said Paddington with a shrug.

"You genuinely don't care about the gold, do you?" Hunter asked. He sounded surprised.

"There are far more important things than gold, Mr Hunter. Aunt Lucy is missing – you'd feel the same if it was Gina," said Paddington.

"She is . . . my treasure," Hunter agreed. He stared into the fire, battling with himself. He could hear Caboto saying, "CRINGY! The real treasure is the gold. DON'T GET SENTIMENTAL!"

"I know what I have to do!" Hunter argued back irritably.

Paddington thought Hunter was talking to him, as he couldn't see the ghost of Caboto. "Everything okay, Mr Hunter?"

Hunter gave himself a shake and tried to ignore Caboto. "Yes. Just, there are . . . expectations from my family," he said.

"Oh, I didn't know you had other family," said Paddington. "Do you see them much?"

"All the time." Hunter looked up. He could see what Paddington could not – that the ghosts of all his gold-obsessed ancestors were gathered around him. They waved in a friendly fashion.

"How lovely," said Paddington, taking another bite.

Hunter shrugged. "You know how families can be."

"Yes," said Paddington. "Well, sort of. The only family I've known is the Browns. And Aunt Lucy. Before that I don't really know. All I remember is my parents died when I was very young . . ."

"Oh, boo hoo!" sneered Caboto to Hunter. "It's a sob story so you give him the gold!"

The other ghosts all chimed in too. The Edwardian explorer warned Hunter, "Don't let that bear steal our gold!"

The missionary said, "Amen to that."

The gold prospector added hungrily, "Maybe it's time to cook some bear stew!"

All the ancestors dissolved into fits of laughter, none of which Paddington could hear.

Hunter scowled at them. "Shh! We can't eat him yet," he said.

Paddington looked alarmed. "What?"

Hunter looked confused. "What?"

"You said something about . . . eating someone?" said Paddington nervously.

"Did I?" said Hunter, trying to ignore his ancestors. "Probably just the altitude."

"Shall we get back to finding Aunt Lucy?" Paddington suggested politely. He leaped up, eager to get on with the journey.

Hunter nodded and gathered his things while Caboto hissed in his ear, "Don't lose your nerve."

"Maybe there's another way?" Hunter whispered, desperate to persuade Caboto to come up with another plan.

"We're too close for you to throw it all away with your stupid FEELINGS!" sneered

Caboto. "Stick to the plan!" He grabbed Hunter by his collar. "You follow the bear, you find the gold, you eat bear stew!" He started slapping Hunter. "Follow bear! [SLAP] Find gold! [SLAP] Eat stew! [SLAP] **BEAR!** [SLAP] **GOLD!** [SLAP] **STEW!** [SLAP]."

"Are you coming, Mr Hunter?" Paddington called out.

Hunter realised that, as far as Paddington could see, he had been slapping himself! He pulled himself together. "Right behind you!" he called. As he left, he picked up the machete.

And Paddington continued on his uphill journey to find his aunt, following her roars.

Meanwhile, on the edge of the jungle, Gina was up a tall tree, searching the jungle with her binoculars to see if she could spot Paddington and her father. Suddenly she noticed smoke rising from the forest!

"Their campfire!" she cried. "It's not far – on the other side of the valley . . ." She followed the line of the river and looked over to the opposite riverbank. "But the bridge is down." She added to herself, sadly, "Oh, Papa . . ." She understood in an instant that Caboto must have persuaded him to destroy the bridge.

The family looked at the vast expanse of water.

"We'll never get across that river," said Mr Brown.

Mrs Brown desperately clutched her St Christopher medallion. "We need a miracle."

At that very moment they heard the buzz of an engine. They looked up to see a small, rather battered seaplane approaching with the words *"The Miracle"* emblazoned on the side! Mrs Brown looked at the medallion, then at Mr Brown. They couldn't believe their luck!

Mrs Bird was waving enthusiastically from the cockpit as the Reverend Mother piloted the plane down on to the water . . .

CHAPTER NINETEEN

THE MIRACLE

As the sun rose over the vast, misty mountain range rising from the jungle, a tiny figure scrambled up a slope through the vegetation. It was Paddington. He roared. Ahead of him on the trail, a herd of wild llamas scattered into the undergrowth. Paddington gasped because, once the llamas had gone, he could see some ancient and overgrown stone steps, winding upwards. And a roar came back in return! Paddington's eyes widened, and he ran towards the sound.

"Aunt Lucy!" he shouted.

Paddington finally burst through the undergrowth into a long-abandoned Inca city, built into the mountainside. Paddington looked at the half-collapsed slabs of stone and the crumbling wood structures. *Was this El Dorado?* he wondered. He gave one more roar . . . and a reply came from inside the maze of ruins, even louder than before! Paddington sprinted along the ancient alleyways, excited to find his aunt.

"Aunt Lucy, I'm here!"

He ran up some steep, carved steps and emerged into a giant stone amphitheatre to find . . . that it was completely deserted.

He spun round in puzzled circles, crying out, "Aunt Lucy?"

But it was his own voice that bounced back off the walls of the amphitheatre.

"*Lucy . . . Lucy . . . Lucy.*"

Paddington gave a long, loud, desperate roar in response. The sound went round the smooth stone structure and came back again as a series of even louder echoed roars.

Paddington's face fell. It was just a trick.

"You mean . . . all this time . . . you were just an echo?" he cried.

"*. . . ECHO . . . ECHO . . . ECHO . . .!*"

Paddington slumped against the wall in despair and sank down to the ground. In his paws were Aunt Lucy's broken glasses, and he clutched them mournfully – the glasses and the bracelet were all he had left of his aunt.

"I'm sorry, Aunt Lucy. You found me all those years ago, but now I can't find you," he sobbed, holding the glasses close to his chest.

A sinister voice came out of the shadows: "So, the bear showed the way."

Paddington found himself looking up at a figure who towered over him menacingly. He gulped back his fear. But, as the shadow got closer, he realised it was only Hunter.

"But if this is El Dorado –" Hunter bent down and yanked Paddington up by his duffel coat – "where . . . is . . . THE GOLD . . .?"

"There is no gold, Mr Hunter. And no Aunt Lucy. There's . . . nothing," said Paddington sadly.

Hunter cast Paddington aside. Paddington fell back in a heap, confused by Hunter's callous behaviour. The man was fully possessed by his greedy ancestor now – Caboto was working through Hunter! But, of course, Paddington could not see this.

Hunter started pacing back and forth. "No. This can't be!" He inspected the wall at close quarters, pulling away dirt and moss, running his hands over it. "There must be something . . . some special mechanism that leads to the gold." He paused, noticing a tiny shred of fabric poking through between two large stones. "Aha! What did I tell you?"

Paddington saw it too and sprang to his feet to inspect the material.

Hunter studied the small white fragment. "Strange Inca symbols . . . a triangle . . . a circle with an X through it . . . 'Dry clean only'?" He sounded puzzled as he read the words on the fabric.

Paddington grabbed the scrap of cloth and peered at it. "It's a washing label, Mr Hunter." He flipped it over and read: "'Barkridges of Kensington'." His eyes widened. "Aunt Lucy's scarf! She bought this in London!" He looked up. "Are you behind this wall, Aunt Lucy . . .?" he asked, desperately hoping his aunt would hear.

Both he and Hunter rushed to try to force the stones apart, but they had no luck.

Hunter began searching for a secret mechanism. "This must open . . ." He ran his fingers over the stones, frowning in concentration. Suddenly he noticed one of the stones was a slightly different shape from the others. "There!" he shouted triumphantly. It had a special symbol on it in the shape of a bear, with slots carved into the rock for its nose and mouth. It looked just like the statue at Rumi Rock and the talisman on Aunt Lucy's bracelet!

Caboto's voice came from within Hunter. "Those clever Incas," he said. "The bear shows the way . . . The talisman! It must go here! Take it from him!"

Hunter fought the idea. He couldn't take Aunt Lucy's precious talisman from Paddington! "It feels wrong . . ." he protested in his own voice.

But Caboto became furious, and his own voice ripped through Hunter. "WRONG? Five hundred years of searching for gold is WRONG?"

Paddington was getting increasingly worried

by Hunter's strange behaviour. He hid Aunt Lucy's talisman behind his back. He watched anxiously as Hunter seemed to argue with himself.

"But I made a promise to Gina . . ." protested Hunter.

"Forget about Gina," ordered Caboto's voice. "Take the talisman. Kill the bear!"

Paddington was horrified. Hunter was now completely possessed by his ancestor and loomed scarily over Paddington. He looked completely mad.

"Give me the talisman!" Hunter roared.

Paddington kept his paws behind his back. "Talisman, Mr Hunter?" he asked innocently, as though he had never set eyes on such a thing in his life.

"Hand it over . . ." Hunter warned in his menacing Caboto-voice.

"No." Paddington stood his ground.

"I said . . . hand it over!" demanded Hunter.

Paddington drew himself up to his full height and bravely said, "Promise we can go in together."

Hunter snarled. Caboto had complete control of him. "The thing about that, bear, is CABOTOS . . . DON'T . . . SHARE!" Hunter clenched his fists, ready to strike the young bear.

Paddington's face was frozen with fear. He gasped, his heart faltering. Would Hunter really hurt him? He held up his Windsorman Deluxe in defence.

"An umbrella?" Hunter scoffed.

"Not just any brolly – the Windsorman Deluxe!" said Paddington proudly.

Then, just as Hunter lunged forward, Paddington clicked the button on the handle of his umbrella and it burst open into Hunter's face, sending him stumbling backwards. And Paddington ran away as fast as he could.

While all this was happening, the Browns, Mrs Bird and the Reverend Mother were all crammed on board *The Miracle*. Mrs Bird shouted back over the noise of the ancient seaplane's rickety engine.

"Apparently they bought the plane for the Pope's visit . . . in 1985!"

"And it's got its . . . MOT and everything?" Mr Brown asked anxiously.

"Mmm, it's got a Papal blessing . . ." said the Reverend Mother.

Suddenly the lights and electrics went out. The Reverend Mother gave the dashboard a loud thump with her fist, and they flickered back on again. Everyone breathed a sigh of relief.

"What's that?" asked Jonathan. He pointed at a ruined city built into the hillside of the misty cloud forest.

Mrs Brown peered through the binoculars. "It's Paddington and he's in trouble!" She could just make out the tiny figure of Paddington breaking away from Hunter and racing off through the ruins. "Reverend Mother, can you land?" she asked.

"I can aim for that clearing," said the Reverend Mother. "But it will be tight!"

There were concerned faces all round as the Reverend Mother made the sign of the cross before beginning her descent.

CHAPTER TWENTY

THE CHASE IS ON!

Paddington skidded to a halt at the edge of the stone steps where he had heard his roars echo back at him. The place was a labyrinth of ancient ruined buildings. How would he ever escape Hunter and find Aunt Lucy? In a panic, he quickly chose a direction and ran as fast as he could. He raced down a narrow passageway, but behind him Hunter had already appeared on some steps, hot on Paddington's heels!

Paddington dashed away from him down more steps, but stopped at the centre of some criss-crossing paths, uncertain of which way to go, then picked one at random. Just as he disappeared from sight, Hunter appeared at another set of steps and arrived where Paddington had been before. Hunter then chose a different route and left, just at the moment that Paddington reappeared! The chase continued with one of them appearing just as the other had disappeared, both of them seeming to get more and more lost in the maze of ruins.

Eventually, Paddington came to a row of openings in the stone that looked like windows. He could hear Hunter on the other side of the wall, talking to him in the scary voice he had used earlier.

"Where are you, bear?"

Just as Hunter's face appeared in a window, Paddington ducked. They followed each other like this along the wall of windows. Paddington thought he had got away and was safe at last, but he had not realised a section of the wall had crumbled away! He crawled past, but Hunter was standing right there, glaring down at him!

Paddington froze. He had to think quickly . . . He placed a loose stone in front of Hunter's feet, then scuttled away. Hunter immediately started after him, but tripped on the stone, and fell flat on his face! Furious, he scrambled back up, and shouted, "Come back with that bracelet!"

Hunter tore after Paddington. But neither of them had noticed that the stone Paddington had taken had left the wall unstable and had loosened some larger rocks. There was a loud rumbling noise as an enormous boulder rolled into view, thundering after Hunter and Paddington, threatening to flatten them both!

Back on the seaplane, the Reverend Mother was preparing for landing. She tugged at various controls, wrestling the plane under her control. "It might get a little bumpy!" she warned.

"It's already pretty bumpy!" said Mr Brown.

A red light started flashing angrily.

"Ach! That doesnae look good," said Mrs Bird.

"The landing gear's jammed!" cried the Reverend Mother. "Someone needs to open that panel in the floor and pull the manual release!" she called.

"Don't worry, I've got it!" Mr Brown leaped over to the panel and yanked it open to reveal a huge purple-kneed tarantula squatting inside. He gave a high-pitched squeal.

"Hurry up, lad!" shouted Mrs Bird. "We need those wheels out!"

"Yup . . ." Mr Brown hesitated. "Does anyone happen to have a . . . very large tumbler?" He was frozen to the spot.

"DAD!" Jonathan and Judy both shouted at him to hurry up.

Mr Brown swallowed. "Embrace the risk," he said to himself, trying to summon up the courage. "Embrace the . . . RISK!" At that moment, he spotted the risk manual and decided to use it to gently lift the spider out. The spider squatted on the book. Mr Brown's eyes narrowed, and the spider stared back. Mr Brown manoeuvred the beast slowly towards the side window of the plane, then used his free hand to unhook the window. A huge blast of wind blew the spider back on to his face.

"Come on, Henry!" said Mrs Brown.

Mr Brown was terrified. "Yes," he said, trying to sound normal. "Just coming!" He turned round to reveal the spider sitting on his face! His family gasped.

"Wait, Dad – let me get a photo!" said Judy, aiming her camera.

"FORGET THE PHOTO!" Mr Brown shouted.

Judy snapped one anyway as Mr Brown reached down to pull the release lever, with the spider still on his face.

The wheels began descending and a green light flashed on the dashboard.

"You did it!" Mrs Bird cried.

Mr Brown gingerly pulled the spider off his face and ushered it back to where he had found it. "There you go. Home sweet home." He slammed the panel door shut, and exhaled, with a cry of approval from Mrs Brown.

"Well done, Mr Brown," said the Reverend Mother. "We're all set now!"

But at that moment the plane flew beneath a banana tree sticking out from the mountainside. One of its huge leaves splatted on to the window, totally obscuring the view . . .

"AHHHHHH!" everyone yelled as the plane plummeted towards the ground.

*   *   *

Hunter was still chasing Paddington, but they both stopped when they heard a deep, rumbling noise. They looked behind them to see the massive boulder rolling towards them. Now they were both running away from the boulder!

Paddington and Hunter raced through a stone doorway and paused for breath. They looked back at the doorway, expecting the boulder to break through when – CRASH! – the boulder smashed through the wall directly behind them instead. They hurried down the zig-zagging path as the boulder pursued them. It was as if they were characters in a computer game. Hunter ducked out of the way, but Paddington was still running from the boulder. He hit a dead end, but the boulder turned a corner at the last second, narrowly missing him.

Then, just as Paddington thought he was safe, Hunter reappeared and tried to grab him! Paddington backed away and toppled off a high ledge . . . Terrified, he found himself falling through the air, but he quickly thought of using his Windsorman Deluxe as a parachute! Thanks to the umbrella, he came to a soft landing on the back of a llama! Paddington realised then that he was surrounded by a whole herd of llamas. In the distance, Hunter was still racing towards him. He had to think fast.

"Excuse me?" Paddington said to the llama. "Could you please, erm, 'giddy up'?"

But the llama refused to move and went back to eating grass instead. Paddington had an idea – he removed his hat and reached inside. The llama stopped eating and sniffed the air.

Hunter was getting closer. "Bear! Give me that bracelet!" he shouted, then paused in disbelief. He could see Paddington galloping away on the llama, which he was "steering" with his emergency marmalade sandwich stuck on the end of his Windsorman Deluxe!

Paddington directed the llama through the maze-like corridors as Hunter sprinted after them. The talisman glinted on Paddington's paw as the llama took him back up the stone steps.

"I'm coming, Aunt Lucy!" Paddington called.

Suddenly, the boulder reappeared round the corner, and the llama bucked, sending Paddington flying from its back, and making the marmalade sandwich fall straight into the llama's mouth. The llama ran off, munching happily.

Paddington picked himself up and raced away from the boulder, down some steps and past Hunter, who had paused for breath as he was getting very tired. At the last minute, Hunter saw the boulder hurtling towards him and leaped aside.

Further down the steps, Paddington narrowly escaped through a doorway that was too small for the boulder to fit through. The boulder smashed against the doorway's wall, causing the whole side of the building to fall in one single movement. As the wall toppled, Paddington was saved. He had managed to stand in exactly the right spot to fit through a window! However, he was now completely wedged in the tight window space, unable to move.

All Hunter had to do was reach in and grab him . . .

Meanwhile the seaplane was descending fast, the huge banana leaf still pinned to the windshield. Everyone was in a panic.

"One of these must be the windscreen wipers!" cried Mrs Bird. She pressed some buttons – one of them blew off an emergency hatch in the roof.

"Stop pressing buttons!" shouted Mr Brown.

"I've got an idea . . ." said Jonathan, thinking quickly. "I'll need backup!" His head popped out of the hatch. He was wearing flight goggles, his fringe billowing in the wind. He heroically produced his new improved Snack Hack invention. In one smooth motion, he activated it, and the extendable hand snatched the huge leaf off the windscreen and threw it behind him. Then Jonathan dropped back down into the plane.

"That thing is ingenious," said Gina admiringly.

"I call it the Snack Hack," said Jonathan. "Patent pending." He slicked his fringe back confidently and looked over to his parents, who nodded proudly.

"This is it!" the Reverend Mother shouted suddenly as the ground veered towards them. "Brace yourselves!"

CHAPTER TWENTY-ONE

ALL IS REVEALED

Back at the top of the ruined citadel, Hunter faced Paddington as he teetered on the edge of a very steep cliff. Hunter snatched Paddington's umbrella.

"The Windsorman Deluxe can't save you now!" he growled, and hurled it into the abyss.

Paddington wobbled dangerously on the edge. "You really don't seem yourself, Mr Hunter!" he said nervously. "You don't have to do this! I don't think you *want* to do this."

For a moment, Hunter's eyes cleared and he seemed to be back to his old self . . . but then his face hardened once more, and Caboto took over again. "I am Gonzalo Caboto," he growled, "and I WANT MY GOL—" He turned, now aware of the roar of an engine. "What—?" He could see the seaplane barrelling towards him.

As the wheels touched down, the plane lurched violently. Everyone and everything inside it was thrown forward – including Mr Brown's risk manual, which flew across the cabin and smashed through the cockpit windscreen like a missile. It zipped through the air towards Hunter and struck him right in the gut. Hunter sank to his knees, crying, "Ooooooooh!"

Paddington's paws flailed frantically in the air as he tried desperately not to fall backwards off the cliff-edge. Then he regained his balance and toppled forward in a relieved heap.

Just then, the seaplane's brakes screeched to a halt. The plane was covered in jungle vines, and the Browns were still crammed together on one seat, their arms wrapped tightly round one another.

Mr Brown noticed his wife had a secret smile on her face. "You looked like you *enjoyed* that!" he said.

"Just nice to all be on one sofa again," she said.

The Browns clambered out of the plane gratefully while the Reverend Mother switched off the engine, unclicked her seat belt and reached up to get her guitar case. She saw Gina looking at her strangely.

"We can all sing a hymn of thanks once we've found Aunt Lucy!" said the Reverend Mother.

But Gina wasn't looking at the guitar. She was looking at the Reverend Mother's forearm. Or, more specifically, the family crest of the Cabotos, which was tattooed there!

"Paddington!" cried Mrs Brown, as she rushed over to hug him.

"I'm so happy to see you all!" he replied.

Mr Brown picked up his risk manual and dusted it down. "I knew this would come in handy," he said, pleased with himself. Hunter groaned quietly.

"I know where Aunt Lucy is . . ." Paddington blurted out. He handed over the torn label.

Mrs Brown peered at it. "'132–137 Kensington High Street'?" she read. "She's at Barkridges?"

Paddington shook his head. "She's

somewhere behind this." He pointed at the huge stone wall, and they all turned to look at it. "And I think I know how to open it," Paddington continued, beaming.

"Clever little bear. I was rather hoping you would . . ." said the Reverend Mother.

The Browns turned, looking puzzled as the Reverend Mother stepped out of the shadows with her guitar case.

"Reverend Mother?" Paddington said in surprise.

She opened her guitar case and produced from it not a guitar but a huge old gun! An ancient blunderbuss.

"What on earth are you doing?" asked Mr Brown.

"Why, same as everyone else, my dear . . ." said the Reverend Mother. "Looking for gold." Her voice took on a touch of ice. "So thank you for leading me right to it. As I knew you would." She aimed the gun. They all raised their hands nervously.

"This is a bit unchristian, isn't it?" said Mrs Brown.

"It would be," said the Reverend Mother, "if I were really a nun . . ." Then she swept off her wimple, revealing a head of long, luxurious hair.

Hunter sat up, a bit winded, but he was back to himself at last. "Cousin Clarissa?" he said, his voice full of disbelief. "But you're dead! You died in the jungle! You went to find yourself!"

"I went to find *gold*. And I never stopped looking." Clarissa grinned. "When I found out the lost treasure had something to do with bears, I did the obvious thing – disguised myself as a nun and got a job at the Home for Retired Bears."

"And to think I played bingo with you!" said Mrs Bird, outraged.

"Years I was stuck there with those mangy fur bags," said Clarissa, her voice full of distaste. "Till one day, Aunt Lucy showed me that bracelet – and I knew that *you* were the one who would lead me to El Dorado, Paddington."

"Why me?" Paddington asked, confused.

"Oh, she never told you?" Clarissa smirked. "It's *your* bracelet, Paddington. It was round your ankle when she pulled you out of the river."

Paddington's eyes widened with astonishment . . .

"If anyone could show the way, it would be you. So I lured you to Peru, and arranged for your aunt's 'disappearance'," Clarissa said with glee. "I grabbed Aunt Lucy's glasses and the bracelet and pushed her away in a canoe, which flowed downriver towards the rapids. I knew you'd never rest until you found your dear Aunt Lucy. And with a little 'help' from me . . . Yes! I was the one who slid the map behind the photograph in Aunt Lucy's cabin for you to find. You led me right here. So, please . . ." She held out her hand expectantly. "Give me the talisman. Thank you."

Paddington checked his paw and did a doubletake. There was no bracelet. He looked aghast and started looking around.

"I don't seem to have it," he said. Clarissa looked furious. "I really don't!"

"Then WHO HAS . . .?" roared Clarissa.

They all turned to see Hunter holding up the talisman.

"Hand it over or I shoot," said Clarissa.

"With Great-grandad's gun?" Hunter laughed. "That thing's over a hundred years old. It won't even work."

"How about we test it?" Clarissa suggested. She tugged on a rope and Gina stumbled into view, gagged and tied up with cargo netting from the plane.

Everyone gasped.

"Gina!" Paddington cried.

Clarissa pulled Gina close, ripped the gag off and pressed the gun to her.

"She means it," Gina said. "And she's very strong for a nun!"

"She's not a nun!" said Mrs Bird.

"The gold or your daughter?" said Clarissa to Hunter. He looked between Gina and the talisman, seeming not to know which he should choose!

"You're all family. Couldn't you just . . . share the gold?" Mrs Brown suggested.

"CABOTOS DON'T SHARE!" Hunter, Gina and Clarissa chorused.

"All right," said Mrs Brown hastily, "just a thought . . ."

Clarissa thrust the gun at Gina.

"Papa! Please!" she cried.

Hunter looked at Gina and saw the disappointment in her eyes. He struggled with how this made him feel. "But I'm so close! I can't lose it now. I've been searching forever in this sweaty jungle. I'm hot, flushed and uncomfortable . . ."

Paddington was giving him a very hard stare . . .

"Why do I feel so queasy?" Hunter asked nervously.

"It's called a *hard stare*, Mr Hunter," said Paddington, "and it's for when people have forgotten their manners and the important things. Gina's your treasure. Don't lose your daughter because of gold."

Hunter considered these words. He looked at Gina – then at the ancestors who were still there, urging him on – then at the wall, and the talisman in his hand . . .

His cousin Clarissa tightened her grip on the trigger . . .

Hunter looked up at Gina . . .

"I'm sorry, Gina . . ."

Gina's face dropped.

Hunter looked up at the crashed plane. It was caught on a branch with a vine wrapped round it. The vine led around the plane and all the way to his feet.

"All I can say is . . ." he went on as he picked up the vine, "boom."

Gina looked back at Hunter, understanding.

Clarissa looked puzzled. "Boom?"

Hunter yanked the vine until it snapped and allowed the tree branch to pivot round. Gina ducked, and it swung directly at the Reverend Mother, knocking her on the head.

"Ow!" She slumped into a dead faint.

In that moment, all of Hunter's ancestors evaporated into wisps of smoke – Caboto last of all.

Hunter ran to Gina, and they embraced.

"Papa! You broke the curse!" Gina cried.

"We're free!" said Hunter. He turned to Paddington and, with great ceremony, handed over the bracelet. "Go and find Aunt Lucy," he said. "I've got all the treasure I need."

"Thank you, Mr Hunter," said Paddington politely.

He held up the talisman. It glinted mystically. He walked up to the wall where the symbol of a bear was carved into the rock and traced his paw over the slots for its nose and mouth. Everyone waited, wide-eyed. Paddington slid the talisman into the nose . . . Then with a pathetic "clunk" the talisman dropped out of the mouth hole! "Oops. I'll just try that again . . ." said Paddington. Mr Brown rolled his eyes. Paddington retrieved the talisman. He blew on it and gave it a "special rub", just as he had done with his coin in the photo booth at Paddington Station.

"I'm coming, Aunt Lucy," he said. He confidently thrust the talisman into the nose slot, and this time it dropped into the device with a satisfying CLANG.

The ground began to tremble. An ancient mechanism engaged . . . The wall rumbled – from deep within, weights and stone gears crunched and turned, dust vibrating out of

every crack, and the entire wall slid open –
revealing a passage through the mountain.

Paddington was about to enter when the
undergrowth around them started to shift and
move. What appeared to be huge plants by the
citadel wall were actually the *espíritus del
bosque* who had been hiding in plain sight all
along. Everyone's eyes widened.

"The forest spirits. They're real!" cried Judy.

The lead spirit growled.

"And they don't sound friendly," said
Mr Brown.

"Quite the opposite, Mr Brown. That was
my bear name," explained Paddington.

It roared again.

"I think they want us to go inside,"
Paddington went on.

The forest spirits stepped aside and
Paddington and the Browns walked into the
passage through the mountain. Then the forest
spirits followed them in, and the huge stone
walls shut once more with a heavy thud.

CHAPTER TWENTY-TWO

TOGETHER AGAIN!

Paddington bravely led the Browns through the dark tunnel, not knowing what lay beyond. Up ahead, there was a dazzling light, just as Paddington had seen in his vision.

"Look!" he said in amazement.

Paddington and the Browns emerged into a vast green valley, which had been hidden behind the stone walls. They gasped as they took in the beautiful sight – the entire valley was bursting with orange trees: rows and rows of them, the brilliant sun shining on them, casting a magical golden glow. Vibrantly coloured flowers grew from lush green bushes.

Exotic birds flew from tree to tree. Waterfalls
tumbled down the mountains on the far side of
the valley into a turquoise lake. And down in
the centre of the valley was a collection of
cosy-looking huts with thatched roofs in the
shape of bear heads!

"Oranges!" exclaimed Mrs Brown in wonder.

"Thousands of oranges!" said Judy.

"And juicy ones at that!" said Mrs Bird.

Paddington was inspecting the fruit, smelling
them. "They're perfect – every one!"

"But what about the gold?" asked Mr
Brown.

"I think we're looking at it . . ." said Mrs
Brown, putting out a hand to touch the fruit.

"Of course! The gold is oranges!" cried Mr
Brown, taking one and sniffing it in delight.

Mrs Brown nodded in agreement, her eyes
bright with happiness. "El Dorado is an
orange grove!"

"Paddington, look," said Jonathan, pointing.

The forest spirits now stood before them in
a line. Then, one by one, they removed their
masks to reveal they were in fact . . .

"Bears . . ." said Paddington in wonder.

One of the bears pointed and growled, and Paddington looked over. His eyes widened as he dropped the orange. And he roared . . . And an answering roar came back to him from somewhere deep inside the bear village.

Paddington immediately broke into a run. He raced down the valley to the village, past a whole tribe of bears who watched him go. Shy little cubs peeked out from behind the legs of their parents as Paddington ran and ran. He hurried through the village square past a large stone statue of a bear. He didn't stop until he reached a thatched hut where, sitting in the shade, on a bamboo chair was . . .

"AUNT LUCY!" he cried.

"Paddington!" she replied in amazement.

He rushed towards her and threw himself into her arms.

"I always knew you'd come for me," she said, hugging him tight.

Then Paddington stopped and remembered something. "Oh! You'll be needing these."

He handed over her glasses. She put them on and saw Paddington properly, and the Browns arriving too.

"My, my! Quite the rescue party!" she said.

The Browns gave Aunt Lucy a massive hug.

"We're so pleased you're safe," said Mrs Brown.

"All thanks to these bears," said Aunt Lucy. "They heard my roars and rescued me."

"Who are they, Aunt Lucy?" Paddington asked.

"And why do they dress up like trees?" asked Mrs Bird.

"To stay hidden," Aunt Lucy explained. "They are the secret guardians of the El Dorado oranges . . ."

"They know my bear name," said Paddington in wonder. "And I've been dreaming about that statue." He pointed at a bear statue in the village, just like the one at Mr Gruber's shop and Rumi Rock.

Aunt Lucy looked at Paddington. "It's time," she said. "Help me up . . ."

Paddington helped his aunt to her feet.

Leaning on Paddington's arm, she led him towards the tribe.

"When Uncle Pastuzo and I found you," she said, "we were so happy to have you in our lives. You told us you were orphaned as a cub. But we always wanted to know where you came from. The answer was with us all along – your bracelet. I kept it safe for you."

Paddington thought for a moment. He looked around at the bear tribe, who were now smiling and nodding at him encouragingly. All the cubs were wearing the same kind of knotted bracelet as his – some on their paws, and the smaller ones wore theirs on their ankles.

Aunt Lucy looked back at him. "All the cubs here have them. So, if they get lost . . ."

Paddington finally understood. ". . . they can find their way home."

Aunt Lucy nodded.

'I think . . . I remember . . ." Paddington looked up at an orange hanging from a tree. He frowned as a vague memory came to him of reaching for an orange, and then falling into a river and getting lost.

"In finding me, you have found yourself," said Aunt Lucy. "They are your tribe – you are an El Dorado bear."

Paddington looked at his tribe. He hesitated, then walked forward to a joyous welcome.

The Browns looked on as the El Dorado bears spoke with Paddington in their native language.

"What do you think they're saying?" asked Mr Brown.

"I think they're just . . . happy to have him home," said Mrs Brown.

Paddington came up to the Browns, his eyes shining with joy. "Mrs Brown," he asked, "would you mind taking these for me? There's something my tribe may enjoy. I just need Jonathan's help . . ."

He handed her his hat and coat.

Mrs Brown smiled, but there was a little sadness in her eyes.

CHAPTER TWENTY-THREE

HOME IS WHERE THE HEART IS

Jonathan used his invention-making skills to help Paddington build a wonderful wooden marmalade-making machine! So, later that day, Paddington and Aunt Lucy were able to cook up some marmalade in a huge stone pot.

"That is good!" said Paddington. "With oranges this wonderful you have to make marmalade!"

Aunt Lucy was stirring the pot, and she let Paddington lick the stick. He nodded approvingly.

The Browns and Mrs Bird watched Paddington and his tribe together.

"He looks so happy," said Mrs Brown. "Like he never left."

Mr Brown and Judy put their arms round her.

"Oh, Mary . . ." said Mr Brown.

"It's all right. This is how it should be. Paddington belongs here," she said.

"With his clan," said Mrs Bird.

Mrs Brown was still holding Paddington's duffel coat. Then she noticed something in the pocket. She slowly pulled out . . . a battered luggage tag. She stared at it and read it. "Please Look After This Bear. Thank You."

She fought back tears, remembering how the Browns had found Paddington all those years ago, sitting on his suitcase outside the Lost and Found department of Paddington Station.

She slipped the luggage tag into her own pocket.

"I didn't realise it was this difficult," said Judy.

"It's just what happens next," said Mrs Brown, giving her a hug.

Paddington came over, holding a pot of freshly made marmalade. Mrs Brown put her smile back on for him.

"This one's for you," he said. He gave the jar to Mrs Brown.

"Thank you, Paddington."

"No, thank you, for . . . well, for everything you've done for me. And . . . um . . . there's something I wanted to ask." Paddington looked at the ground awkwardly. "You were all so kind to take me in all that time ago . . . I know it couldn't have been easy . . . and that I've sometimes been a bit of a nuisance. Sorry about that business with your pyjamas and the paper shredder, Mr Brown."

"That's all right, Paddington," said Mr Brown.

"So, I wanted to ask, if you didn't mind terribly, if . . . um . . ."

Mrs Brown tried hard to prepare herself for what Paddington would say next. All the Browns were trying to keep it together.

"Yes, Paddington?" said Mrs Brown. She waited, barely able to breathe.

Paddington swallowed, plucking up his courage.

"Could I come back home with you?"

Mrs Brown's eyes brimmed with tears as she took this in.

"Of course, you can, Paddington! You don't need to ask that. I thought you were going to ask to stay here."

Paddington looked at the other bears, then back at Mrs Brown. "Mrs Brown, they are my tribe, but you're my family. This is where I'm from, but you're where I belong."

Mrs Brown and the rest of the family smiled with delight and relief.

Paddington cleared his throat. "There is *one* more thing I wanted to ask . . ."

EPILOGUE

Paddington had persuaded the Browns to let his El Dorado cousins come to London for a holiday! They loved staying at number 32 Windsor Gardens. The Browns were a little worried about the wisdom of having so many bears to visit, as the house was full of chaos – but also joy. There were bears sliding down the bannisters and stampeding up and down the stairs, while Mr Brown's desperate pleas of caution could be heard.

"That was my mother's!" he cried as they accidentally knocked a vase from the hall table.

Paddington and his cousins charged up the stairs into his little attic room.

"And this is my bedroom – from my window, you can see all of London," Paddington said proudly.

The bears looked around, amazed, and then stampeded away again.

Paddington took them on a sight-seeing tour of London. They squashed together into a pod on the London Eye, caused a rumpus in a teashop and posed like the Beatles pop group as they strolled across Abbey Road! They even had a takeaway from Jonathan's favourite chicken shop, the El Dorado.

When they got back to Windsor Gardens, several cubs tried to have a bath all together! They filled the bath with too much water and when they jumped in they flooded the bathroom. Paddington smiled. *I was like that once*, he thought fondly.

Meanwhile, back in the Home for Retired Bears, Aunt Lucy was having her breakfast. She took a bite out of some toast and El Dorado marmalade and settled down to read a letter. (Her glasses were now thankfully repaired.)

Dear Aunt Lucy

*It seems a long time since our holiday
together in the valley and everyone's
lives have changed so much since then . . .
It's good that Mr Brown was able to
sort out the insurance for Mr Hunter
and Gina, and they now have a new
boat.*

*I gather the Church forgave Clarissa
Cabot – providing she became a REAL
nun and took a new posting. Apparently,
she ended up in the Arctic, working at the
Home for Retired Polar Bears. I don't
think she was very happy about it!*

*As for the Browns, it seems as though
Jonathan has given up "chillin'" and is
hardly ever in his room . . . He spends most
of his time at trade fairs now, doing
something he calls "hustlin'" – the "g"is
silent. He has shown his inventions,
including the Gobsleigh and the Bicy-chill,
to some businesspeople who were very
impressed.*

*Mr Brown has been promoted at work
and he is now Head of Calculated Risk.
He showed everyone a slide show of
Judy's photos from their time in Peru and
included lots of pictures of himself in
dangerous situations. He told them all
about the purple-kneed tarantula landing
on his face and said that some risks are
worth embracing, but only if they're for
the greater good. And for the people you
love. Apparently, everyone clapped in
appreciation. He finished by saying that
he was doing a sponsored parachute jump
for the Home for Retired Bears – and
then he did the jump there and then, out
of the window!*

*Mrs Brown has been working on a new
art project called "Taking Flight". It's a
beautiful picture of a flock of birds, spread
across the sky above Windsor Gardens.
And, despite her previous fears, she's
actually closer to Judy now than ever. The
pair of them have been playing "Scrabble*

with Friends" while Judy is away at university. Judy's travelogue about her time in Peru got her accepted on to her favourite journalism course, by the way, so she is already hard at work "setting the world to rights". She has also been writing an article for the student newspaper. The editor told her that she had done good work and that, with a few changes, the article could make the front page. Judy was thrilled, but was less pleased at the prospect of "changes"!

I hope Mrs Bird is enjoying her stay with you, and that she's ticked a few things off her new "to-do" list. She told me that she was going to install a mirror ball and disco lights in the main hall. I can just imagine her as the Home's DJ . . .

As for me, I think I made the right decision. Mr Gruber was right when he told me you can have "mixed feelings" about where you're from. But maybe that's okay because I suppose I am a bit *of a mix. Part London, part Peru, a sprinkle of El Dorado . . . But most of all – a whole lot of Brown.*

Love from,
Paddington
(also known as ROOOOARRRR Brown)

ALSO AVAILABLE: